# MATCHBOOK

# MATCHBOOK

*John Dempsey*

Iriswhite Publishing
North Carolina

# Matchbook

Iriswhite Publishing
North Carolina
For information, visit www.iriswhite.com

ISBN: 0-9711072-5-4
Library of Congress Control Number: 2004118295
FIRST EDITION

For recidivists, dipsomaniacs, and hotel room demigods ruling from stained sheets at 9 a.m. on a Sunday.

# TABLE OF CONTENTS

## From *Steps To The Madhouse*

## From *The Progress Of Ants*

# MATCHBOOK

The guitar, drums, vocals came hammering, pulsating, wailing loud and fast, hard enough to make the windows shake, a speaker blow, a glass break, loud and fast, a jackhammer popping and exploding in our eardrums, enough to wake a baby, enough to send momma running for the crib while fumbling a titty from her dress, enough for the young father to storm into the room with envious eyes on baby slurping and sucking away on that pale white momma titty, damned baby monopolizing breast and stretching cunt and sucking up all that sweet momma attention when it should be focused on . . .

"Turn it off! Turn it off!"

"Why?"

"Oh my god! How can you listen to that?"

"Because it's my new favorite song."

"It's terrible!"

"It's amazing! It energizes me! Makes me want to move and do something crazy!"

"You're always doing something crazy."

"But this is different. It makes me want to reach across and punch you in the mouth!"

"John!"

"It makes me want to punch myself in the mouth!"

"What's…"

 "When I hear this song I can run neck first at a plate glass window."

"Did you just see that guy cut me off?"

"If I had guns I'd point them at my crotch and shoot my nuts off! Shove a grenade in my ass and pull the pin while sitting in traffic!"

"Why did I get in this lane?"

"That's the kind of music I like. Music that makes me move and react. Music like a catalyst! Like a hormone!"

"What was that?"

"A whore moan!"

That's how I want to write, loud and fast and hard enough to make me react. Sometimes I'll type something that seems so wild and dangerous that I get shakes up and down my arms, legs, spine and if no one's looking I jump out of the chair, pull and tug at my dick, bang it against the keyboard until I'm satisfied, spell check it and send it off to a journal, a magazine, an anthology, tape it to the inside of my thigh and hop on a bus to Fort Lauderdale . . .

"O.k. The turn should be coming up right around here. Keep your eyes open."
"They're open! Red! Open! What am I looking for?"
"It's a banquet hall, Panama something or other."
"I think I know it. Panama Jack's. Their logo is an old British guy in a Panama hat. He's got a bicycle handle moustache, a monocle, and he's smoking a pencil thin cigar."
"Are you sure about that?"
"Definitely, I could never forget that face. Homosexual, pedophilic, aggressive; one hundred percent predator! Rabid wolf with a hard-on. Semen foaming at the mouth. Hyena jaw crunching down on young boy shoulder blade, back of the neck. Priest's outfit and a confessional booth. That's our guy alright."
"What's wrong with you? I don't think…"
"No, no, it's true, I wouldn't make those things up."
"Yes you would. How can you talk like that?"

I think it's got something to do with dying twice a week and the calendar whispering Tuesday, it's only Tuesday, while rolling across the carpet, and there's elves, dancing up and down the walls, singing Christmas tunes, sharpening razors, they've got fangs, those damned cheerful, malicious smiles, an overdose of ringing bells, a semi-death, the small kiss, the cliché *Hard to learn, easy to master* . . .

It takes years of playing hero, villain, poet, racecar driver, masturbation artist, sharp shooter, stunt man before taking that first . . .

Semi-death
a 10 year mountain of emptied beer cans of cigarette burns of ripped letters of hotel rooms and runny noses and window ledges

sending invitations and speeding trains throwing dance parties
mama . . .

I lead with my right foot on third rail tap step pharmacy counter
double shuffle open veined bathtub blues lock the doors and
disconnect the smoke detector, I've gotten my hands on a match.

One of those white-headed, strike anywhere . . .

*Hard to learn, easy to master*
a 10 year mountain of semi-deaths and false starts and not
enough sulphur to light a twig let alone
set the place on fire . . .

"Well just get it out of your system before we get there. I don't
want you saying these things in front of my co-workers."
"Don't worry honey, I've seen these guys before, they're not
looking for…"
"You're right, they're not looking for anything. Just act normal.
Don't talk about grenades or whores or wolves. If someone says
something to you, I want you to stop and think before
answering."
"Yes mum."
"And only 3 drinks."
"What?"
"You heard me, I don't want you getting drunk."
"I can have more than…"
"Oh no you can't. You've been eating vicodin all day and it
makes you belligerent when you drink on them."
"Don't tell me what it does, I'm the…"
"See what I mean, and you haven't even started drinking yet."
"Well . . ."

I've been drinking since 12 and I've been a perfect gentleman all
day. In fact, I've been a perfectly dead and rotten corpse of a
gentleman since I woke up at 7 this morning itching, feverish,
crazy from a thousand dreams of semi-death in a small room . . .

*Hard to learn, easy to master*
years of playing secret agent, cowboy, pervert, journalist,
student, executioner, suicide case, dead man before taking that
first . . .

*It's all downhill from here boy*s
add another 10 feet to the 10 year mountain of semi-deaths; I've
been strangled, drowned, gutted, shot in the back while running
across dream fields, slipped on ice in dream alleys, cracked my
skull against imagined dumpsters, jumped from dream roofs and
painted the street pink, tumbled down stairs from one dream to
the next, a thousand dreams, 10 feet, I lay in a pile of broken
neck and no feeling at 7 a.m. in my dream bed holding a match .
. .

One of those diamond-tipped, strike anywhere...

"Follow that car! Quickly!"
"What are you talking about?"
"That guy in the white Honda just took a picture of me! He
looked Asian!"
"Please John, all I'm asking for is 3 hours. Just behave for 3
hours and then you can do whatever you want."
"But he was Asian. Don't you know what that means?"
"Yes honey, I know what it means, we'll get him later, I
promise. Now, if you behave tonight I'll give you a present."
"Ooooh. What kind of present? Is it candy? Head?"
"I can't tell you. Just be good and you'll see."
"Is it a hand job? A striptease?"
"John."
"Yes mum."
"Stop calling me that! Now you get nothing."
"I'm sorry, I'm sorry, from now on . . ."

*It's all downhill from here boys*
a collector of matches of semi-deaths of scars of stitches of
literary pyromania chasing poetry off fire escapes, a 10 year
mountain of fingers trying to strike a light, strike a light and with
each death a new spark, a smell of sulphur, a small flame,
another match . . .

One of those bulls-eyed, strike anywhere...

*And soon enough*
I lead with my right foot on third rail pharmacy counter double
shuffle lock the doors and . . .

"Alright, finally. Now John, remember your promise."
"I know baby, I'll be good. And then I get a present, right?"
"That's right. But only if you're good the whole time that we're here."
"Of course. And I can have 4 drinks now too!"
"We'll see. It depends on how you act."
"Oooh. I'll be so good. You won't believe your eyes honey."
"I hope so."
"Just wait, you'll shit your party dress!"
"John!"
"You'll piss all over yourself with surprise and love!"
"John, why do you have to start everything like this? This is my office Christmas party. The least you could do is try . . ."

*And soon enough*
third rail pharmacy counter double shuffle roll up the windows and lock the doors I've gotten my hands on a . . .

Matchbook


## ❧ A BEAUTIFUL NIGHT


find myself with a 7-foot European and the bastard grandson of Ernest Hemingway.

the bastard grandson has just completed his first novel,
he gives me a copy. the 7-foot European orders a round of drinks,
he gives me scotch-whiskey
with soda, the bartender forgets my lime - fucker.

I'm cursing in gutter Arabic at a 6-inch Mexican. guy's standing on the pool table, blocking the 8. I sprinkle him with words not spoken
on this side of the globe,
chalk up,
and knock him across the bar with my cue.

there's a young brunette,
makes me think wet

sloppy
drunken
thoughts - tangled legs, lots of moaning, I scratch on the 8 and
finish my drink.
get into the bathroom.

standing at the urinal, I hear a noise behind me. turn,
see the lid of the toilet bowl rise,
and the 6-inch Mexican jumps out. guy's covered in shit,
holds a tiny little gun, yells
"Fucken Mariposa!" and puts a bullet into my gut.
I notice a wet spot on the leg of my pants - urine - walk out
with a paper towel pressed to my stomach,
and that paper towel is magic. thing can change colors, goes
from white
to red
in no time at all.

I buy the next round,
ask for a dollar in quarters and slam them down on the wooden
lip of the pool table,
knock off the scotch-whiskey with soda
plus lime
in one heroic gulp, scream
"who's fucken next!"
and
pass out.

## ෫ CLOSE CALL AND THE RECOVERY

This is my
nine a.m.
beer prose,
red eyes and the future's

bright, Saturday morning and I've been at this since Thursday
night: mix 4 hrs sleep with 2 cases of beer, 3 painkillers and 50
dollars of weed - I'm a goddamned beautiful

stumbling

mess. (When the test came back positive, I was sitting, alone, in
a rented apartment, midtown Manhattan with the t.v. on (I even
remember the show, *Fact or Fiction*) and it was a stock letter, to
whom it may concern, from the medicine men at this ultra
upscale
clinic; the New York City Department of Health & Mental
Hygiene (half the people in this neighborhood get tested there).
And I had plans that night to meet these two redheads for drinks
but
that no longer
seemed like an option.

The letter fell outa my hands and sailed down to the floor just
like a nice little death notice should.

And my heart rate was all punk rock drumbeats. And there was
(lightening) one thought running destructive through my brains:
I'm dead - DEAD - I'm a fucking
dead man . . .

I sat that way for some time, maybe an hour, maybe more, seeing
the future: bed sores and decaying immunity, hospice services
and a frail young man shaking helpless with disease. You see,
I've always known that something would catch up to me,
something - but, not this - this was too much. This was too BIG -
too FINAL! There was no turning back from this. No "Road to
Recovery." And I picked up the phone and called the two
redheads. Told 'em that I wouldn't be able to make it tonight,
I've come down with something,
rather nasty, sorry and we'll have to
reschedule (yeah
right,
not on this side of life) sorry, and it's o.k. John, cause you don't
sound so good right now, you sure you're alright? Of course
honey, just a little virus, be fine in a bit, don't you worry bout
me. And after I hung up I pulled the jack out of the wall and
turned off the t.v. and walked steady towards the closet because
that's where salvation resides. That's where the
Absolute Escape Dream

lives. The Ultimate Escape Dream.
And I can pull it all off with a simply sick twitch of my pink
trigger finger and right now,
that seems like
the best

idea.

About a year and a half ago I had picked up this .38
snub-nosed special when I was real paranoid off coke. I thought
that this would protect me from the DEA, the white coats, the
regular john law and any other fuckers I had screwed with at
some point or another. Like Kenny Wingtips, for instance. But
the opportunity
had never presented itself.
Shit.
I had never even fired the thing, just toyed around with it,
scaring friends, posing in the mirror type thing. But now, I had
purpose. I had a game plan. There was a reason for pulling it out
and I held it at arm's length and clicked off the safety and I
stared at all that
shiny metal
killing power
and I knew, I fucken knew, that this was my only choice, no
other way out. The Complete Escape Dream. Complete Escape.
No questions asked and no answers given, the next step "Oh
honey,
won't you smile nice for the camera's
blue flash . . ."

And I even wrote out a will, all my possessions, any cash
generated from the writing or insurance plan should go directly
to the blonde. The one with the silk smile and the understanding,
almost motherly,
mind; she could read me
when everybody else seemed illiterate - give it all to her,
I doubt it would be anything, but still. Give it to her, she
deserves it, at the least. And with that done and tied with bakery
string round my neck I checked to make sure I had fresh shells,
(because you psyche yourself up only once to pull something
like this, only once, and if you don't do it,

right off the bat, with no catches, then you'll never do it, that simple). So I'm there with the will and mindset, ready to swallow gunpowder explosion and let one bullet of freedom blare final through my brains and be the end all to end all - Ready! Completely fucken ready, all systems go, prepare for the final liftoff you rotten fucker and this is the only way out.

The
only
way out.

And I've got that wicked
blue steel taste in my mouth, ready to push the final envelope and I realize, that maybe,
I should have that death notice letter wrapped snug round my neck, as, well, as kind of a warning, a statement, a message to the children sort of thing telling them to wear condoms and beware of loose women and long
drunken

bad decision making nights where the mornings are questions of who did I fuck and why did I fuck her/him (no) and did I at least strap rubber round my ridiculous cock with it's eager face spitting white deadly conclusion in it's perfectly circumcised sex drive? This is serious. Pay attention assholes, this is the last real predator! We've

killed everything else that can fuck with us.

Pay attention!

I grab the death letter
"Prepare for takeoff!"
both documents ready and sweat on my forehead, big steps here, giant steps, pay attention, and I take my last look at this place, man, I've lived like a nut job for the last how many years(?) and now
it's all gonna end. Grand Finale! Right here and now, all set, fingers tremble and these are my last thoughts, should I, maybe, think something prophetic? Something conclusive and critical,
something

to be the end all
of end all, and
you know what I wound up thinking about? Whether or not they
spelled my name right on the death letter. You know?
Cause that's been
a perpetual problem of mine.
They always spell my name wrong - letters from social service
agencies and debt collection agents,
they always get my name wrong and I was thinking about how
foolish this would all look, if I pulled the big trigger and
splattered my literal guts across this room and maybe people
would think that it was all over a
misspelled name -
a simply
misspelled name. And so I checked to make sure that all the right
letters were there. That they were all in their right positions and I
noticed a

rather

queer thing: the letter
was addressed to the guy in 4G.

I'm in 4H, in fact,
I run out of the place and check the door. 4H. It's right there.
4fuckenH! Baby-baby governor calls
on my way to the lectric chair
and who says you only live once(?) - I smiled. There was a gun
in my hand. A gun. What was I doing with a gun? 4G! 4 fucking
G.
There were two sheets of paper tied to my neck. 4G.
Do you get it?

Full-Pardon.

Escape from the Escape Dream.

Do you get it? I switched the safety back on the .38,
put it in the closet and folded the death notice letter back up, just
right, like it was
never opened, gripped, twisted the door knob and walked down
the hall - mail slot hello, this is no longer my problem. I pushed

that letter right through the slot and walked away - a million dollars
worth of second chance and I got back in my place, plugged the
phone jack back into the wall and called the two redheads. (I had
plans for the night!) This is my
9 a.m. beer prose,
red eyes and the future's

bright.


## CR YEAH ...


Drank:

dewars and coke with a 7 foot european
at the Pig & Whistle
somewhere round Hudson, by the water and I remember
there was 5 beers with the blonde
on a black couch
stroking her ass and the television was on but
she fell asleep and I took shots shots shots
with two soft fuckers at Off The Wagon and they were all
butter ass
and man tits
no balls
but dollar bills and
big grins and me on the stool, big thirst, eyes slit,
the new york
city host with numb nose
and dark grin
guitar thoughts
on a Friday night, 2 joints
and a little hash, half a valium
about 30 minutes back
and not a yawn - and there were a few lines,
sucked up,
off the urinal in the bar,
and that makes a damn fine surface (white cocaine drip sweet as

pixy stick sugar)
with the brain all
mad sparks and high speed
blood rush, heart like a
jackhammer and 14 cigarettes, twelve cans of bud
on a Friday night
and
oh yeah I'm
headed places.


## ℭ WHAT THE HELL IS THIS?


hey, you think these days get any softer?

feathers to razors
a pillow of steel spikes
finding comfort in broken glass and two drops of whiskey
I wrap my Saturday night
in a white dust coating

I crush my long lost love
between two folds of paper
I snort my warm and pink heart
through a rolled dollar bill

```
        -

      -

    -
```

upstairs

it's known as red-neck heroin

down here
it's a deck of fifty-one

so simple and plain - so damned easy to see
how a man could get caught
become tangled
and lost
in these soft white minutes

in these powdered
sugar
minutes
the gentle clock ticking
the lion draws the shade,
turning round in a circle,
he offers us his asshole.
I find my head buzzing

thinking of Perry Farrell
and of William S. Burroughs
thinking of

Sherlock

Fucking Holmes with his sweet tin of snuff - I've got this MTV
mind,
a Fox Five mentality,
I've got a cartoon upbringing and the highest of aspirations -
none of us

will be here by sunrise

none of us
will do a thing with tomorrow -
me?
I've been inhaling this shit
going on
something like forty hours now and it's a light
reminiscent of ketamine
type haze

the slow mind
the glazed,
suspended,
ultra focused eyes -
I stare at one object in the corner of a room
and it doesn't matter what it is,
could be a stuffed bear
or a blueberry muffin,
could be another line or a bloated corpse,
could be a silver griffin with condoms tied round it's neck and

gold plated crotch rot sipping gin eating crab cakes while young
virgins slip out of their robes and lay naked upon splintery altars,
thighs quivering,
there's the reek of
anticipation,
there's a full moon through the window,
a man in a mask
runs hungry with a dagger, only 4 miles to New Haven
and my love like a drowned man . . .
it doesn't matter what it is,
it brings me enlightenment - you smell my fingers?
Knife on the kitchen table?
Mother left for work and tied us up in the closet?
None of us
will be here by sunrise

none of us
will do a thing with tomorrow . . . I take this poetry shit
way
too seriously.

# CR #1

#1 was a short brunette, she had beat cancer at 18,
and I found her online -

a 6 month courting period and we met up -
The Fat Black Pussy Cat, West 3rd.
drinks until 2 - last call
and we walk outa the place:

"Oh Johnny, I really wish I could bring you home with me, but
my husband and . . . well,
you know."
"Yeah, I know sweetie."

I know it all,
dark streets
downtown Manhattan -

I know an empty phone booth -
I know violent lips - fingers
reaching out for warmth,
my belt undone - I know - my dick in the moonlight, moaning, as
the white
shoots out from my midsection -
I know - the smile on her face,
a real big
Ginsu knife smile, full of sharp teeth
and she gives me this look - real animal like -
I know - she sticks out her tongue (picture of a gazelle
drinking from a pond)
and licks her palm - I know -
smacking lips - water to a woman
dying of thirst - I know -
lighting a cigarette,
watching her slip out of the phone booth
and disappearing around the corner,
yeah,
I know alright.


# CR #2


#2 was head over heels for the bathroom screw sessions, 12 in
the afternoon,
the last stall,
of a third floor men's room,
a high school on Long Island
and we're both just 16 and we're both just
too dumb
with lust
to really care -

in the woods behind her house - our jackets on the ground and
the snow in our eyes,
I found my way
-in-

my parent's station wagon - middle of a parking lot, in the
backseat, I found my way
-in-
the elevator
and on the train
-in-
a Laundromat,
and behind a gas station,
once in a tree house
and once in a tool shed
twice under the boardwalk, on this stretch of beach called the
Sand Hole, and the second time around was the last time around
because we noticed ticks while getting dressed and I'm afraid of
ticks, deathly afraid, and so I screamed and (shut up john!) they
were burrowed into our asses and I screamed and in our arms
and (I can't think with you yelling like that!) our legs and I
screamed and on our necks and we stripped back down to
nothing (someone's gonna come if you keep making all that
noise.) and I screamed and we stood there naked (shush!
someone's here.) and I screamed while we burned them off with
flaming match heads and (hey, what the hell are you kids doing
down there?) they sizzled and I screamed and (my parents are
going to kill me!) when they burst and (more people) the black
lacquered blood from (hey, get out from under there.) their black
bloated bodies sprayed (I hate you!)
in a fine mist (never again!)
across our tanned skin, well,
I screamed then,
too . . .


## ↱ 20 DEGREES IN NEW YORK


not a writer
not an artist
I'm Houdini with a keyboard - 20 degrees
in New York,
and I'm brain dead,

sitting in a 5th floor office; I'm listening to guitar concertos,
I'm half-stoned,
head nodding
to Bee's Moonlight Sonata,
it's Monday morning
and up next
is Segovia

not an author
not a painter
I'm an astronaut without a rocket - 20 degrees
in New York,
and I'm brain dead,

sitting in a 5th floor office, I'm sucking on two tabs of valium,
I'm listening to Boyd
play Bach
on a Tuesday afternoon, I'm warm,
wrapped up in an eggshell,
as Malmsteen
is queued

not a musician
not a bull fighter
I'm barely
a real person,

I'm just an addictive personality
that's read too many books - it's 20 degrees
in New York
on a Wednesday morning
beer binge,
I'm dreaming
with my eyes open, listening to Vivaldi's Largo,
acid rain in Amsterdam,
Harmonic Inspiration, the whole world a jail cell,
and me
. . . an escape artist.

# ⊂⊃ (AND I SEE MYSELF . . .)

I'll be 39 in January - But you look about 27, what's your secret
- I don't drink much,
don't smoke,
exercise a few times a week and
maintain a healthy diet.

(I see him being hit by a car,
face up in a coffin,
looking about 27.)

I'm 45 and I jog 7 miles every morning - You must be in great
shape - Yes, steady heart rate, strong legs, I sleep well at night
and I never feel run-down.

(I see him slipping on a train platform,
falling back onto the third rail,
those big strong legs
jittering high voltage jig.)

I've been lifting weights since I was 16 - Strong Man - I can
bench 250 pounds, throw a discus over 200 feet
and in High School I took All-State
for the 50 meter dash.

(I see him arguing with a stick-up man,
bright muzzle flash, bloody on a street corner,
dead at 35.)

I've been drinking beer since 8 this morning - Drunk and a Dead
Man - I've smoked half a box of Marlboro,
and 2 bowls of resin,
masturbated twice,
and drawn cartoons across my belly.

(And I see

myself

living

forever.)

# ℭ 3 A.M. Waiting

on one line, one word, one
anything. Meanwhile,
outside,
there's something hanging round
there's something painting the walls
there's something grinning at the window
and laughing loud in the rain.
It's always that damned rain.
Damned rain will make you feel
like the fall-apart kid,
a few flashes of poetry
and then disappearing
into the milk easy night.
You drop so simple, while
waiting on brilliance
to knock down your door
to grab you by the shirt collar
and pin you to the machine. Meanwhile,
inside,
there's something stuck
there's something stuck between a rock
there's something stuck between a rock and a hard place
and that something
is you, damned
fall-apart kid
with your few flashes of poetry
and your milk easy night. Question: What're you going to do
when the brilliance doesn't come? When that one line, one word,
one
anything doesn't come? Answer: The only thing that you can do.
Type something like this
and
wait.

# ‫CR THE FIRST FUCKEN SNIPPET

I'm the captain crunch kid, snorting 2 hits of Dexatrim, Thursday
night and I just bought an 18 pack

I'm Billy fucken Gates, electronic cock in my hand, Thursday
night
and I'm down to 16

Last year
I was the tale of brave Ulysses, I slapped this one brunette in a
downtown bar and fought a Chinese kid on the A train, Thursday
night
And I'm closing in on 14

Tonight
I was drinking at Fritz's on Hudson with the 7 ft European and
he told me that if I quit my job I'm one stupid fucker cause I got
benefits and brains and upward mobility jet type propulsion
blasting hell fire out my ass, plus
I play guitar, Thursday night
with a twelve and there's no way I'm seeing the 925 come
Friday

twelve thirty-nine in the basement of my parents house,
Oyster Bay,
Long Island I'm wearing blue jeans and budweiser, hives play
punk, the 21st century, I woke up in Huntington and hitchhiked 6
miles to the market where its 12.39 for 18 beers and I think I'm a
real fucken somebody in my Amsterdam t-shirt with 8 beers
rattling in my fridge

I call my girlfriend,
she's this hundred pound blonde that tells me some people are
actually going to work tomorrow (love you baby) and I full
moon witch cackle raising hairs on your neck pour half of this
beer on my face and throw the phone against the wall, Thursday
night a six pack
and when I die at 28
you fuckers better remember me (I'm 25 now)

pause for cigarette and beer run, Thursday night
riding a ten speed to the 7-11 cause some smart fucker took my
car keys - give me a few minutes, I'll be back


## ◯ THE SECOND FUCKEN SNIPPET

Thursday night and I found my car keys
Started black-pickup-truck and blasted hard rock punk above the
speed limit

Puked twice on my way to the store and yes
I've got the decency to open the door so as not to get it on the
floor mats, shit, (who wants blood and bile on their floor mats?)
I'm refined
a real gentleman, super renaissance
modern day
all class
type you'd introduce to your parents
type kid

another 18 beers spell my name in shiny letters

(Shit!
Never explained the Dexatrim - here's how it works,

two words:

Snort everything!

When you're speed balling bathroom coke and shit-grade xanax
you might as well crush up a few diet pills - speed -speed does a
body good, Thursday night
typing bad poems
and I swear to god I'm the missing link)

a chicken bone dress suit - if I were a designer
that's what I'd design
an entire suit made out of these polyurethaned chicken bones and
I'd wear it
everyday - sprinkle angel dust on my brains and a propane
enema - why not? Thursday night with the top down and I shave

my pubes, do that trick where you tuck the shaft between your
chicken legs, makes you feel real weird, like maybe, you're
kinda fucked up, not right
somehow

Thursday Night Fuckers

3rd nipple growing outa my elbow (it's really a wart) and its just
plain freaky, specially when I play guitar with the thing,
specially when I play good guitar with the thing - they ask,
is that a talent
or just disgusting - not sure, its Thursday night, deewee suicide
case while giggling real troll like, gnome under the bridge like -
anyone wanna bring me flowers? 4 beers down and another 14 to
go - I'm stepping out
getting high on 20 dollars worth of green bud
- be back

(of course you'll be back, you're a fucken junkie to this shit. If
you don't type
then you're dead inside, it fills you up, it's your food, you eat it,
you live it, fuck!
You breathe this shit and without it you'd suffocate - I know,
(that's me speaking)
and that's why I said
I'll be back) (sorry, sorry,
multiple personalities, reality constraints, sometimes I'm unsure
as to who's what around here . . .)


## ‿ THIRD FINALE – ENOUGH OF THIS SHIT


Back at it -

no more Thursday night,
I'm edging into Friday morning with domestic beer and lunatic
smile plastered cross my face

(what the fuck is this thing? - one continuous flow,
this thing is a real-time journal entry without censor
or coherent thought

this thing is my thursdaynight/fridaymorning guts laid open for
the vultures-peck peck-feels good-keep pecking-release process-
better than ejaculation-peck peck-freedom shoots like white
globs,
aims at the stars,
closes my eyes)

allows me to type like this,
fingers like a hurricane and I remember how in high school I
won this one award for a short story I had typed up on acid
(Jesus Christ?) and it was about a dream I had had (word games)
where I was a stretch of sidewalk and all day long suits and ties
would walk reckless across me and I would pick up

vibrations

from their steps, aura type vibrations that gave away
their insides -
(Showed 'em in a real rotten light) fighting with the wife, for
instance, and the hands fly wild, black eyes and the awkward
mornings, fingers in the twelve year old with sweet smile (See
those hips? Henry the fifth?)

and I was surprised to win the award,plus 25 dollars to the local
bookstore,
or even graduate (regents diploma and college credits with a
coke habit and this bitch of a girlfriend that had this sugar pussy
- got me on all fours, face buried in pink and coming hard), it's
Friday

morning and I've got 8 beers to my name,

I'm down to resin at quarter 2 three
and I think I'm Antonio Banderas in *Desperado* -
trained guns
painting holes in the opposition
and there's no way
that this shitty little poem
can go on
any longer

# ✆ 12 IN THE AFTERNOON

and the camera finds me
hanging round in front of Canterbury's (can't smoke inside, not
anymore) already half-cocked,
on beer since the a.m.
with this kid (poor fuck's enlisted in the Reserves, I think)
smoking rolled
and filtered
Turkish tobacco and the kid's mad to be stomping on quiet town
streets (kid would
trade it all in
for the desert
and the sweat) but right out front of Canterbury's is a bench
and that thing's positioned just right (sun and trees, birds, no
wind, that whole
tranquilized
summer feeling, warm air, the beach, barbecues, beer rolling in
your
stomach and there's
no thoughts of allies or coalitions, robots, fruit flies or
deadlines, timetables or schedules, just this bench,
that's it, and all you gotta do is sit on the thing, just sit) but
with the current state of affairs
the kid's not interested, he's dreaming of something
uh,
a little more liberating,
a little more heroic
than all this and he finishes his smoke
and runs back inside the bar (they've got CNN in there,
they're televising the biggest damned reality show of all time
and I think it's real fucking scary) then a leaf shakes free from
one of the trees, a car drives by and honks twice at a young girl, I
get up and walk three blocks north,
for some reason,
I don't feel like going back inside.

# ❧ CRIMINAL INTELLIGENCE

Monday morning with stains on my shirt
there's a white face belonging
to a 3 handed executioner
there's numbers like years
drawing out a jail sentence
there's messages waiting
like a jury's *guilty* verdict
and while I sit here chained
to a desk dreaming of tunnels
or of slipping unseen
into the back of a laundry truck
the smartest men of my generation
are gathering together in the sun
to roll dice for cigarettes.

# ❧ A CHOICE ENCOUNTER, A MOMENT
## OF ENLIGHTENMENT

ordered a beer
and sat down.
next to me was a mass of gray hair
and gray beard
some flesh
some blood
some bones
a few teeth.
guy opened up a hole in his face and puked out three words,
"burn it all."
a brown bottle slammed down in front of me like some nose
diving jetliner.
I looked at the big board and it flashed.
the big board flashed train departures and train arrivals,
track numbers

and destinations. I was in a bar, I was in Penn Station, I was in New York,
with 20 minutes to kill.
the mass turned in my direction and puked all over my shirt,
"burn the trains, burn the commuters,
burn the busses, the subways, burn New York, L.A.,
Washington, burn Alaska,
burn it all."
I sucked at foam.
it bubbled up the bottle's neck and slid down the sides.
"burn the banks, burn the schools, burn the hospitals,
burn all the computers, microwaves, and wristwatches,
burn it all."
I drank half the beer.
my shirt was covered in puke and the big board flashed track 21.
"burn the police, burn the army, burn the national guard and the
air force, burn Time, burn the nine to five,
burn your family,
burn it all."
there was puke on my pants. it dribbled in chunks down my leg
and splattered off my shoes.
I finished the beer.
5 minutes till take off,
still thirsty, New York,
sitting at a bar in Penn Station,
I signal the bartender for another round.
"burn Christmas, burn Valentine's Day,
burn Hanukkah,
burn it all."
another jetliner crash-landed in front of me.
I was thinking of how the foam was like smoke,
the red label was fire,
all that golden liquid inside was the trapped souls of all the dead
passengers and I was like some great mouthed god accepting
them into my body.
"burn the telephone booths, burn the automobile plants,
burn the jails, burn the supermarkets,
burn it all."
I was covered in puke.

people walked in and out of the bar but always in a circle around
the puddle that had formed on the floor beneath me. my train
was boarding on track 21, a bar in Penn Station, New York,
three words, one thought,
"burn it all."
I turned to the mass of gray hair
and gray beard,
the mass of some flesh and some blood and some bones,
the mass of few teeth,
and asked what he was drinking.
he lifted a short glass,
swished around the half a sip of liquor that sat at the bottom,
and puked,
"whiskey."
I waved over the bartender,
ordered two glasses of whiskey,
and looked at the big board.
I had another 20 minutes to kill.


## ᏉᏚ SATURDAY NIGHT IN MANHATTAN


found myself on west 46th street, between ninth and tenth
avenue, walking with actors, producers, musicians,
dancers and the blonde
and in the hotel we changed into pants, shirts, skirts, shoes,
chewed vicodin
and smoked a bowl
then we were at a street fair where I picked up Ian Flemming for
50 cents
and a silk shirt for 3 dollars - the blonde found a bracelet but the
man wanted 7 and I said 4 but he just wouldn't budge and so
when another customer walked up I put the thing
in my pocket - back to the hotel
so we could drop off our purchases
chewed more vicodin and smoked another bowl,
off to the restaurant,
Italian with the pre-theater menu and two bottles

of good white,
sun was just going down and on the street after dinner I was hit
with a bad case of the wine sweats, back to the hotel - showered,
redressed, then on to the show,
the Richard Rodgers Theater
where a man tore our tickets into halves and turned us loose
inside, where the beer was 4 dollars a can and water was 3
dollars a bottle and you were only allowed to bring water into the
theater
so you spent 7 and dumped the water into a toilet then filled your
bottle with the beer - expensive - then the lights went down,
a man played a piano 10 feet off the ground,
another man kissed a saxophone, a guitar kicked in
and Russians flung themselves across the stage,
pirouettes, muscled calves,
so much water in a lake and I clapped after the first act then ran
out for a beer -
intermission,
outside, smoking cigarettes on the street with models and
spectators, photographers like big game hunters
and this one guy with 8-inch long nails and a digital camera - the
nails were all well painted with landscape scenes of tree and
grass, ocean, dancing women, exotic birds -
snapping pictures of stockinged legs from the ground up and
catching bright billboards in the background,
a red uniform yelled
"Curtains goin up folks!"
and we streamed inside and up the stairs like salmon,
refilled my bottle and sat down for the second act,
the wine, beer, vicodin mix sweetening my thoughts -
after the show we were in an outdoor bar off second avenue with
large Roman columns and overpriced drinks,
I saw a man that I swore was Jim Morrison
and another guy that had to of been Ken Kesey, but I might've
been wrong, who knows, we,
the blonde and me, drank vodka with soda till 3
then caught a cab,
back to the hotel, stripped to panties, boxer shorts and shirts, we
climbed out onto the fire escape to smoke and watch the sky,

3 stories below us cats hissed and fought,
bums crawled into doorways with whiskey derelict dreams while
store owners turned down their lights
we finished our cigarettes, stubbed them out on the fire escape
grating, maneuvered back in through the window and got into
bed,
laying there under the covers,
the air conditioner whining,
she turns to me, says,
"I really wish you hadn't stolen that bracelet, John. It's going to
come back to you one of these days."
and I grabbed her in the dark, pressed my face into her neck
smelling all that good summer time smell that came off her skin,
kissed hard
and said "Maybe."

## CR AND MY LOVE, LIKE . . .

I was on the couch, 4 fingers into Friday, when the phone rang:

Mr. Dempsey. Yes. Do you know who this is? No, can't say that
I do. Well, I know who you are. Oh yeah? Yeah, and I just
wanted to let you know, we've been watching you.

Watching me, huh? (And the scenes flash through my brain: 12-
year old Navajo girls in wire cages down by the seaport, 3
bundles of dust lay under my mattress, an unlicensed Luger sits
in my closet, that fire in the park, standing with two 50 dollar
blondes, eating Reds and pouring gasoline. I turn to Friday "It's
time to go baby. Daddy's got work." She huffs, gives me a look
and walks outa the place.) That's right John. We've accumulated
quite a file on you.

On me? And what exactly do you have in this file?
Everything.
Everything?
That's right. All of it. Every bar fight, every drug deal, all the
girls you've been screwing, those dogfights you used to have in
the basement. Nothing escapes us.

Shit.

Shit is right, and I just snapped some more pictures of Friday. You shouldn't have told her to leave; she's one fine piece of ass. Yeah she is, you should see the tits on her, she's all woman that one.

I know, I've got pictures man, oh boy do I have pictures! Last weekend was more of a porn shoot than anything else. How in the hell did you pull off that standing 69? I was impressed.

Thanks man. It's all in the shoulders, you gotta distribute the weight just right so that . . . Wait a minute; you've been taking pictures of me, 69ing with Friday?

Yup, we've got you standing up, we've got you in the shower with her, on the train with your old boss, in the laundry room with Maria. Like I said John, nothing escapes us. Ab-so-lutely nothing.

Hey man, who the fuck is this? Why are you following me around and taking pictures?

John, that's for us to know . . .

And for me to find out, right?

Wrong, fucker, you'll never find out. Just know that we're watching you.

Oh yeah, then what am I doing right now?

You're pinching your right nipple using your left hand.

Fuck!

Haha - Take it easy buddy. And keep screwing!

I hang up. Start inspecting the place. Microphone under the desk lamp, 3 wireless video feeds: living room, bedroom and bathroom, I unscrew the phone receiver, see a 470 Ohm 1/4 Watt Resistor, a 100V Ceramic Capacitor, a 24VDC Reed Relay, and I know what this shit is. A bug. I take one of the wireless cameras, drop my pants and aim the thing at my balls. Now that's Film damnit, yelling at the bug. Then I flush it down the toilet, pull up my pants; slip the cameras and microphone into my pocket, head out the door.

5 blocks away is the Pawn & Loan. I get 250 for the spy gear and there's a trench coat with black gloves trailing my ass. I've seen enough movies to know what this means. I walk outa the Pawn, quickly, 2 blocks North and slide into an alley, pick up an empty

bottle, blackberry brandy, duck behind a dumpster and when the trench coat follows, I blind side the fucker.

An hour later: I'm back at the apartment. Trench coat is laid out on the couch, garbage bag ties wound round his wrists. I sit backwards in a chair, sucking on beer and looking through his wallet. His wallet tells me the following: Patrick J. Evans, Private Eye, licensed by the State of New York, pistol carrier's permit, 5 foot 10, 230 pounds, 38 yrs old. There's also a picture of a brunette and little boy with similar features. I light a cigarette, take a swig of beer, and spit it into the trench coat's face.

Ughhhh
Hey Patrick.
Ohhhh.
Up and at 'em Patty boy.
Huh?

I get up off the chair, swing an open hand - flat smack echoes off the walls and the trench coat flashes awareness - red handprint - blood from the corner of the mouth. I settle back into my seat.

Ok Patrick - time for 20 Questions. You ready?
Fuck you Dempsey.
I'll take that as a yes. Question #1: Why are you following me?
I said fu... (and I don't even let him finish, in these types of situations you gotta be tough so as soon as I begin to hear that "f," I'm outa my chair - backhand across the mouth brings more blood and I feel like I'm in control of the situation).

Ok Mr. Evans, lets try this once more. Why are you following me?
Because somebody hired me to.
And who's this *somebody*?
Look man, I really can't - (I get halfway out of the chair, that's all it takes) - Broody . . . Broody.

(Night of the Living Dead - overturned tombstone - ghosts walk the street - fast motion video of clouds and sun and moon dancing through the sky - my love like a drowned man, bloated, floats up to the surface . . .)

Did you say Broody? (5 yrs together)

Yeah, she called my office about 7 months ago. I've been tailing you ever since.

And reporting back to her?

Yeah, she wanted to know everything, who you hung around with, women in your life, whether you had a job or not, all the details.

Are you serious?

Yeah.

Ok, you got an address on her?

I don't know man, I can lose my license for giving out that kind of - (I give him a look and the dick starts singing. An out of state address and I see travel plans in the near future - a pilgrimage - *I'm leavin on a jet-plane* (home is where the heart is) *don't know when I'll be back again* - and my love like a drowned man . . .)

20 minutes to pack, I leave no forwarding address, Mr. Evans sports duct tape and dried blood around the mouth. I promise him freedom in about an hour "A buddy of mine will come by and let you go, but remember asshole, I know where you live, try anything and I'll come back for you." I make the street, black duffel bag slung over the shoulder, 300 dollars cash, 3 bundles of PCP, a copy of Fiskadoro, by Dennis Johnson, and my thumb in the air.

LaGuardia Airport, LGA, 1-way ticket, Florida, and no, this bag has not been out of my possession since I packed it, no, nobody has asked me to transport anything, yes, and yes and please and thank you.

Uneventful plane ride, 4-dollar cocktails at 12,000 feet, I knock off the Johnson book, not bad, pretty damned good actually, then take a nap. Wake up in Orlando, 85 degrees (oh mamma) and my love like a thirsty man (I'm home) stumbling through the desert.

65 dollars for the Grey Hound Bus Line, 150 miles to an apartment building in Sarasota - home is where the heart is - destroy the heart and the man is no more - Night of the Living Dead - oh mamma, your baby has come home an amputee - I roll half tobacco, half dust into a thin joint and smoke the thing behind one of the parked busses. 3 hours - angel dust dreams -

the streets curve below, beneath, behind, beyond me - time like smoke - burns like incense - *so kiss me and smile for me*

Dusk on a Florida street - *tell me that you'll wait for me* - apartment #7G - *hold me like you'll never* - and I don't even ring the bell.
I stand at the door. 30 seconds later, she opens up.

Holy shit!
Hi honey.
John, what are you doing here?
Looking for you, didn't the dick fill you in?
The dick?
That private eye, Evans, the one you hired.
No, I haven't heard from him in a week. How'd you know about him?
Baby, that guy was second rate; I caught him following me around last night.
Did you hurt him?
No, no, just pulled some information, how do you think I found you?
Oh . . . well, so now what?
I'm not sure yet, (there's so many times I've let you down) but I do know that I haven't stopped thinking about you once (so many times I've played around) in these last two years (I tell you now).
And what about all those girls you've been with? (they don't mean a thing)
Honey, there are women in Miami, New York, St. Martin and Mexico, but not a one of them, can turn a step with your grace.
John, all that poetry is fine and all, but you catch anything since the last time we were . . . you know?
No, I'm pretty sure that I'm clean.
You sure?
Well, there are 2 zits on my ass.
Let me see . . . Ok, turn around . . . You plan on staying here?
Where else would I go? (so kiss me and smile for me, tell me that)
I've got some condoms, (you'll wait for me, hold me like) make sure that you use one tonight. (you'll never let me go) We'll get

you a physical in the morning.
Oh baby, you have no idea how good it feels to see you. (and my
love like a groundhog, no longer afraid of its shadow . . .)

## ℭℜ DOWNTIME IN THE DEAD CITY

Peaks and valleys,
I've hit a slump.
Downtime in the dead city,
not a decent line in six months and
"Captain,
no sight of land on the horizon!
Empty blue space up ahead and our reserves have run low.
Even the rats have jumped ship!"

Vultures
have replaced them.
Damned dead city birds
can sense failure 20 miles away and their nose
has led them to my home.

They rap on my door with dead city talons.

Words dribble from their beaks
and like some good mother
I can recognize my children anywhere -
stillborn poetry
picked out of a dumpster behind the clinic,
chewed and spit up
by these dead city birds roosting on my doorstep.

I've got two choices:

I can open the door
and let these dead city birds into my home
or
I can load the handgun
and step outside to meet them.

I pull the Dempsey mask from my closet
along with the .45 caliber Firestorm,
step out onto the doorstep, take aim,
and type these dead city birds
right out of existence.

## ○ℜ DISCONNECTED FROM LATE MAY

speedball off quaaludes and coke
taper off on 20 milligrams xanax and 10 cans domestic beer
sunday morning, 2:30
my numb face slides around on my round skull and drips
drips down towards the chest area, cheekbone on the shoulder
nerve endings on strike, the nose has called it quits, relates a
state of incommunicado,
has joined forces with the conglomerate coalition of Brain, Body
& Backbone, Inc. "John,
shutdown is eminent.
Self-Destruct sequence initiated and probability of survival is
12%"
Best possible alternative:
2 shots Absinthe (merchant marine type acquaintance, name of
The Fugitive,
guy smuggled a bottle in from Italy - Ernest,
I know), half a gram of hash, and then fire up the bathtub - 2
liters gut rot
King Charles scotch-whiskey
19.99 for the large plastic jug - poured about 2 pints on my chest
and let that whole diffusion,
osmosis,
alcoholic that's read too much about the old Romans,
and a few too many
science journals,
figures why not? Strip down and wrap a white bed sheet
toga style
warm water, there's still Church (25 dollars a gram, new york
prices) in the bowl and I pull two hits

watch pinstriped fish weave about like second rate drunk drivers,
problem is that they're floating,
mid air, about 6 feet off the ground and shit, hits me that I might
just be hallucinating.
I twitch a couple of times.
Shake the head and neck,
flex shoulders and straighten the back. 2,
3 deep breaths and open the eyes wide -
wind up in the kitchen,
towel around my waist and boiling a glass pipe -
kid came by the other night with herpes outbreak around the lip
area - saw the fucker take a couple of hits off my bowl and that
set me on edge - paranoid about blisters and puss drool out my
mouth - I had a pot of water bubbling and the resin was leaking
out of the bowl. The residue was a brown tea that smelled like
crushed soybeans mixed with peppermint schnapps. I drained the
mess through a coffee filter, filled about half a glass,
stirred in 2 spoonfuls of sugar
and drank the thing down.

Some time around three I was puking.
Leaned up against a toilet I let go a mix of resin tea, stomach
bile, broken down chemicals and high proof alcohol -
half-hour of exertion and the bloody mucus
grand finale.

It was 4 o'clock.
I was in bed,
head spinning, flashes of nausea, cold sweats and dry heaves,
there's a window in my bedroom
and 2 solid knocks had me looking through the glass.

Fucker Paul the Shape Shifter. Reason I call him that is because
each time you see him he's a different person: Mondays Paul's
in the gym busting ass and building quadriceps on the treadmill;
Tuesdays the guy's outfitted in glo-sticks and double wide pants,
guy's eating x and fingering underage club clits; last Thursday I
saw him in the passenger seat of a 2003 Cadillac, black-suited,
gold-chained, guinea bull horn and the hair grease, Paul the
Shape Shifter.

Needed a place for the night and I had a couch. He was in a
pinstriped button down; collared round the neck, and a pair of
80-dollar pants with razor's edge creases. Looked like a young
exec type.

Guy had a brown vial of clear liquid with a chunk of white rock
sitting at the bottom. I took 4, 5, who knows, maybe 7 huffs and
settled into a droning, strobe light, brain wave
sort of haze . . . after that, I really don't know, I wound up in
front of a computer.
I was listening to Garcia and typing the night with my eyes
closed,
I was typing with the brain on standby and a soul in limbo,
thinking about a woman,
it was quarter to 5,
and these fingers (damned
autonomous,
revolutionary
fuckers)
have just typed my death sentence.

The sun was up,
might've been 6.
I was up on the roof feeding bits of stale bread to sparrows,
crows, one blue jay and there was a small hawk flying circular
patterns about 50 feet above me.

I started cooing, making birdcalls, shrill whistles, till the hawk
landed.

Behind me was a pump rifle that shot arrowhead pellets at about
250 feet per second . . .

My hands were shaking. Heart rate was something that most
people would've been concerned about. I forced every part of me
to relax, set the hawk between the crosshairs
and got lucky.

Hawk took one right under the wing. Shrieked like an old
woman falling down a flight of stairs and rolled, kicking,
twitching and screeching off the side of the roof.

Got down there and saw him struggling.
Hawk had the look of a soldier that's stepped on a landmine.
Lying there,
dazed, death's head grin visible and something along the lines of,
Doc,
I can't feel anything down there,
but I'm warm, it's my back, Doc, it feels warm - I used the butt
end of the rifle.

Got back inside,
I was a little disappointed with myself, un-sportsmanlike, also
felt light-headed. Fell onto a single mattress and passed out . . .

(I was walking down a Long Island street, passed a gas station, a
softball field, a large yard with Lilac bushes, and while smelling
the Lilac, I tripped over something. I took an amateur boxer dive
and barely missed cracking the front row of my teeth. I looked
behind me; saw a large duffel bag, the culprit. I got up and
opened the thing. Jaw became unhinged, pupils tripled in size. I
saw large bundles of Thai-Sticks, quick estimate of 50 branches,
each branch made up of at least 10 sticks tied together. I began
filling my pockets, bulging, and still there was more. Then I saw
something beneath the Thai-Sticks; bills, 20-dollar bills, stacks
of 'em, 2 grand a stack and I shoved them down the waist band
of my boxer shorts, shoved a stack into each sock, lined my
shoes. I almost had the whole mess, and then underneath the
remaining stacks I noticed something moving, it was jerking
around, I heard a mewling noise, something was alive down
there. I cleared the bills out of the way, throwing them over my
shoulder, I didn't even care, and when I finally got down to the
bottom of the bag, I sort of stopped breathing. Felt paralyzed,
speechless, not a logical explanation - looking up at me from the
bottom of the bag was that damned hawk, fine, the hawk, but the
problem was that it carried my mother's head in its beak. My
mother's eyes were open and they spurt red streams across her
cheeks. Red coursed down the tunnel of wrinkles across her
neck. They would drip off and were beginning to pool beneath
the remaining length of her neck bone. The eyes stared at me,
held me, alive, the lips moved, there wasn't a voice box, it had

been lost, nothing to push the sound out, but still, I heard a word, Karma . . .)

I snapped awake. It was 3:15 in the afternoon. I called out, no answer. Shape Shifter had taken off. I took a piss, brushed my teeth, thought about jacking off, but just didn't have the energy. I needed a shower and coffee. The phone rang. I let the machine pick it up. Fucken telemarketer. I got under the shower and cleaned myself up, gagged twice while brushing my teeth, took a few large sips of water, took some time to recuperate, read half of The Last Tycoon . . .

Round 7 that night I came to the realization that I was a sponge. Kettle One, tonic and a lime had me primed like some top-of-the-line gleaming muscle car type of chrome engine; unstoppable, unsurpassable, not an auto in this yard has the capability to compete. Long as I keep the sponge soaked, the spark plugs'll fire delivering close to twice the energy needed to sustain movement,
you know what,
screw movement, acceleration, that's the key - chemically engineered and custom designed plugs'll produce twice the energy needed to maintain acceleration.
With the right fuel I'll have half the gang beat around the 2nd lap of the Lit 500 - Dictionary Dependant
Cannon Ball Run . . . ah,
meanwhile, I didn't even have plates on the car,
inspection is 4 months expired, and you get a stripped fan belt squealing when you make a right turn, screw it! I picked up the phone. Pulled a number out of my memory and told her to come by,
"Don't show up empty-handed."

Hour later she was there. Quart of Puerto Rican rum, 2 liters of soda and 4 pink pills ((things'll speed a man up to about Mach5) I had her half-drunk, jittery, chemically restless and told her that she had nice legs - took 25 minutes or so) 10 white pills ((to slow the same man down to about Mach3) I poured 2 glasses of rum and splashed in some soda, asked her if she had ever seen my Dali reprint, it's right down the hall, first door on the right - 40 minutes had gone by) and a handful of purple footballs ((to make the mornings a lot easier) yeah, I just got one of those new foam mattresses, check it out - 15 minutes passed by in oohs, light bites, pinches, got the knees running parallel with her ears, wormed, worked, wriggled my way in…)

While she snored I chewed footballs and settled into this hammock I had run across the living room. Thing was 10 feet off the ground. I had also hung a set of speakers from the ceiling. Lying in the hammock they were pointed dead center at your ears and created an odd, reverberating, surround sound effect. For some reason I started to pretend that I was on a space shuttle. I was floating through space and picking up transmissions from alien life forms. The Aliens were named after rock bands and they seemed hostile. I heard them call out for a 7 Nation Army. Shit! A quick appraisal showed me a small cache of firepower. No way I could hold my ground. I wrapped my hands into the mesh of the hammock, shifted my man tits and gut for propulsion, and rolled off into the great…

10 feet…

There was something wrong with my shoulder. Felt disconnected, unattached, screwed up. Plus the side of my head. Lump like an old time cartoon where Fred Flintstone gets the club for staying out late. I wasn't bleeding though, wasn't coughing up blood and no signs of discoloration. Indestructible! I was a damned powerhouse. Damned nuclear generator. Fuck LIPA. Fuck Con-Ed. I'm gonna neuro-bio-electro-fit outlets along my temples and spinal column, run 115 Killa-John's of unbalanced junkie juice, plug every fucker with a lick of enlightenment into my own personal infection zone - they'll wake up with Van Gogh sores and a yellowish Monet discharge, one guy'll go into homo-erotic arrest after mainlining 50 cc's of Billy Boroughs, another fucker's worn his fingers down to the second knuckle, got the Mozart itch and a Korg keyboard, had this one fem in a beret and no bra (nipples were sitting, giving paws, rolling over, good girl, now beg for attention) she was twisting hips on a coffee table while reciting di-Prima. I looked around my little fantasy world. Shit, I felt like a real somebody.

# ❧ FOR ALL YOUR GREEN DREAMS

For all your green dreams
of an easy future in a small town
of circumventing the globe
in some crystalline cruise ship . . .
For all your big business plans
of stock options and cd's
of long term investments
and money market upswings . . .

I offer you this:

(Allow me a moment to pull the scene together:
2nd floor of a semi-decent American chain restaurant. Ceiling
point of view, the camera looking down on a young couple.
Their plates half empty but they've put down their forks to point
across the table at one another, make gestures to emphasize the
words pouring out of their red faces. A man with the *Vision*
would look at them and walk wide circles around the table.
Black Widow aura's deadlier than the bite itself. Camera zooms
in and we've got ringside seats, sitting amongst bread crusts and
spilled beer, a technician in a studio reaches out and fingers a
control panel, takes a dial marked *Audio* and turns it way up, the
sound hits with a crash, and we find ourselves in the middle of
the young couple's conversation.)
"It's just that I don't think you understand the value of an
education. People would kill to be in your position."
"Understand? Who the fuck do you think you are telling me
about what I don't understand?"
"Don't get nasty!"
"Understand she says. Value of an education she says. Shit. I
graduated college with a 3.77 major fucking GPA! I was on the
Dean's List and got my Regent's diploma senior year of High
School!"
"That's not the - "
"Shut up! Let me finish. Bitch! In 5th grade I was in the Young
Astronauts' Club and my model rocket flew the highest and the
farthest of all the rockets built that year, thing went a thousand

feet up, sprung it's parachute and landed picture perfect and it was painted jet black plus had my name stenciled in on the fuselage! You ever do that? No! Before I even started the 3rd grade I had read an entire set of Charlie Brown encyclopedias 4 times over and I had the cock of an ox!"

"But -"

"So don't tell me about education or understanding."

"But it's exactly that. You never think about the future. It's always what you did. What you've accomplished in the past. You don't understand what it's going to mean down the line if you go back to school now. Let me ask you something, just where do you think you're going to be in 5 years? Huh? Have you ever thought of that?"

(And at this point the waitress comes by to see about dessert. She might not have the *Vision*, but she's a waitress, been doing it for a long time and can read people. These people are in for something dark. That's what experience tells her. They'll most probably just want the check. They'll pay in a hurry and walk out leaving her a small tip. Something dark. But when she asks if they'd like anything else, the young woman jumps up like she's been waiting for just that.)

"I'll have a peanut butter fudge sunday please."

"And you sir?"

"Nothing, thank you."

(She clears a few plates off the table and walks out of the scene, only half surprised - something dark - then heads towards the kitchen.)

"So?"

"So what?"

"So, answer me seriously, where do you think you're going to be in 5 years? Working at the same shitty job making the same shitty money? Still dreaming about all the things that you've done in the past. Just living day to day?"

"I don't know."

"Cause I'll tell you what. I don't want to be 40 in a trailer park. I don't want to struggle all my life. I want to be comfortable. I want to be able to buy a house and have a family without worrying about making ends meet. Do you even have any money in your savings account?"

"No."

"Have you ever even tried to save any money? You know what, don't even answer, I already know. You have to really start thinking about what you want to do with your life. Look, you work at a university, a big name university where you can go to school for practically nothing, just take the GMAT's with me this year and see if you can get in. I know you could do it if you wanted to. And I'm not saying that you have to register for any classes, I'm just asking you to try it."

"No, I know what you're saying. I know exactly what you're saying. You're just like all the rest of them out there. You genuinely think that you can change me. You think that you can take me and turn me into something that fits your plans, well, I'll let you in on something, you'll never change me, no one will ever change me. And all this bullshit about futures and comforts and not wanting to struggle, do you have any idea what the greats -"

(Again with the waitress, she sets the ice-cream sunday down and pulls two spoons from her apron, gives the young couple her warmest smile and says "Enjoy." Something dark. But maybe they'll leave a decent tip.)

"I'm not trying to change you. I just want you to think about the future. About our future."

"I'm the fucking future! You really believe that 4 years in a classroom is gonna make all your dreams come true? That you'll get your degree and then all the magic doors of the world will just open up for you?"

"You know, you really have to grow up a little."

"Don't tell me what I have to do. You've just been hanging around with all your little cunt friends and hatching all these little cunt plans for me. Regardless of what they tell you, I'm not one of their weak-kneed boyfriends. I won't be moved by all this, this, pamphlet reasoning on how to plan for the future. Shit! Just who do you think you're dating here?"

"Maybe I don't know."

"Damned right you don't know! If you did then you wouldn't be pushing all this at me, trying to pressure me into these tight squeezes."

"That's not what I'm doing."

"Yes it is! That's exactly what you're doing and I won't stand for it. I won't have you or anybody else telling me what to do or how to live. I'm my own fucking man damnit! I set the pace! I call the shots and I say what's next!"

"I think you should leave."

"What?"

"I said, I think you should leave, you're being loud and everyone's looking at us."

"You think I fucking care? That I give a shit what all these cocksuckers are looking at? And what the hell are you crying about?"

"Because you're being nasty. Why do you always have to be so nasty when I try talking to you?"

"Because you're making me mad. You make me want to flip this table. You make me want to throw this bottle across the room and break every fucking window in the place! That's why!"

"Please leave, please, just -"

(And decency forces the camera to pull up. The technician hits the volume and we're back on the ceiling, watching the young man pull some bills from his pocket and fling them across the table. He storms out of the place with heads turning to watch his progress. The young woman sits at the table, swirling the ice cream around the bowl with her spoon, wiping at her eyes and nose, embarrassed, upset, wondering (how much should I leave the waitress) why she ever started up with him, (10 dollars should be enough) he'd always been stubborn. Unpredictable. And somewhat crazy, yes, he was always a little off . . .)

For all your green dreams
of paths and plans
of rose gardens and trails
lined with polished Belgium blocks

. . . I offer you this.

## ❧ GREEN LIQUOR

in a flask sent to me by a woman in the Midwest
wormwood and 75% alcohol . . .
it's the wormwood that gets you,
11 p.m.,
a fishing dock,
the wind coming in off the
Long Island Sound,
sweeps through the bay and
hits you with a hair dryer similarity,
max power,
feels like an arid desert wind; warm, dry
(I don't know how, but it is), and swaying,
the elbows give support,
the mouth spits laughter, not a fish, not a bite, just green liquor,
a flask,
11 p.m.,
on a fishing dock . . .
it's the wormwood that gets you

## ❧ CLOSING TIME

with the clouds like giant
gliding white elephants
and the car like some fine
tuned European driving machine
and the sun dripping golden
brown honey dipped in fire
with the clock reading six
thirty four in the a m
I realize that I haven't slept
in over 48 hours

# ❧ 48 Hours, For 49 Words,
## Behind The Scenes Of Closing Time

**(Part 1)**

not sure what this is
or where it is
either, might be a dream or hallucination, but I doubt it
I think this is more of a running tally of a running narrative
an account of an experiment
an experiment in itself I'm
sure,
rub cocaine on my gums
and send me out to box a
7 foot Nigerian I'm
still young enough to be dumb enough to
be
damned near
invincible . . . gives me the freedom to experiment . . . makes it
easier to be a human cannonball . . . when there's nothing left for
you on the ground,
being shot into space
doesn't seem all that bad . . . wax wings and a heat lamp . . .
day's darker than the darkest of pygmy rainforest nights . . .
it started last Tuesday night
Wednesday morning
playing cards I drank beer, vodka, wine, smoked 2 bowls of
brown weed and won
50 dollars,
I called the office 7 hours later and let them know I wasn't
coming in. I went to the beach -
I went to the beach with a kid who wore glasses and he made one
joke too many (not
sure what he was joking about,
just that
it was one too many) and when we finished with the beach we
had crab cakes and beer at the beach cafeteria and then back to
the car -

In the car he took off his glasses to wipe at the salt sea spray
accumulation of white particles that had accumulated and I
knocked his front teeth far into the back seat . . . (I receive a
flash of insight some
pink mechanism screams
BALANCE . . .

I imagine two kittens one black one white yin-yanged in the
cutest
of locked genital licking positions . . .

picture wild Dali landscapes of clocks and cocks and women and
sand . . .

recall this one time with this one friend eating fried chicken out
of the bucket on the road and moving
at a sedate
23
miles per hour when alongside of us pulled this maroon auto
with 3 girls with
3
big bodies
huge bodies
of mass
and
eye glint semen dream through the window betrays and big
trembling triple chin quiver with the memory of 3 thousand
white jazzy come runoffs betrays
that these three were out looking to stud . . .
And our mouths full of chicken,
and grease on our faces,
we both picked up that bitch in -
low bellowing cattle in -
screaming striped raccoon in -
yellow yowling cat under your window in -
large pink folds so ultra damned sensitive in all this -
even the flies and jellyfish in air underwater understand and can
tell -
a scent we've become attuned to -
something released by wetly hidden glands in the asshole when

in -
heat.

And I was driving

with the last of a chicken leg in my hand while my friend rolled
down the window with vegetable oil crumb greasy smile
and . . .

"You ever screw a fat chick?"
"Me, nah, not really. A couple of meaty ones, but never a real
big one. You?"
"I was thinking about it this one time. Could've had three of
them. But instead we threw chicken bones and gravy at them
then took off.")

Strange memories on this dying summer day . . .

I left the kid with the glasses in the parking lot at the
beach . . .

I went home and microwaved a tomato . . .

I watched an appendectomy on television and imagined the
doctor to have these old, rummy drunk nervous, unsteady hands
and that he sliced the life right out of the somebody
under the sheet . . .

I dumped out the ashtray in my car and came up with a mixture
of roach papers,
black ash, resin chunks, coke flakes and mushroom stems -
exhaled the first hit after a full 30 count and knew I wouldn't be
sleeping -
took another and crawled under my desk with a steak knife and a
flashlight . . . carved half this monstrosity on the wall using
microdot Sanskrit knowing that no one around this place would
ever be able to decipher it . . . mixed paint flakes and saliva in
my belly button . . . made a chalky paste and spread it under my
eyes around my neck over my
legs . . . found an expired train pass and sang lullabies about
Bulgaria . . . there was something eating away at me . . .

**(Part 2)**

Thursday morning . . . we jump past the 24 hour mark . . .
with a brain more jelly than brain . . . mind more of a reactionary
machine than a thought box . . . I crawled out from under the
desk and into a rectangle of sunlight coming in thru the window
. . . I was feeling guilty about the kid with the glasses and I
closed my eyes for a moment . . . the phone rang . . .

"You piece of shit!"
"What?"
"What's wrong with you?"
"When?"
"I can't believe you did that!"
"What?"
"Don't play stupid! I talked to James!"
"When?"
"This morning. And he told me what happened at the
beach . . ." (I should've maybe mentioned
that he's her cousin, James,
the kid with the glasses
and more than that,
she's my girlfriend . . .)

"Why would you do something like that?"

"I don't know honey, he got me all crazy, he was saying all this
shit, things about you and me and, I couldn't control myself."
"Well, you're going to have to apologize to him."
"Alright, alright. But I took off tomorrow. And I say tonight
we're doing something fun."
"Like what?"
"I don't know yet, something."
"Alright. Wait a minute."
"What?"
"Why aren't you at work?"
"When?"

It then hit me that I wouldn't be going to work anymore
furthermore
I decided that I was in a
rather fragile

and sensitive state of mind, for instance, I thought of screwing
Italian girls from New Jersey with acne scars and genital warts,
girls that listen to Bon Jovi songs and know all the words, girls
that don't mind giving head in strip mall parking lots with
mothers and children milling around holding shopping bags, not
the usual things a man should be thinking about on a fine
sunny
Thursday morning.

I took a shower and made a phone call . . .

. . . black man's alleys . . . real estate, you douche bag, it's all
about location, a million open noses per square block . . .
bandannas, sirens,
gray, gray, gray . . .

I took a long beer lunch at a Mexican place over on 8th - 2.50
pints - then talked to the book vendors across from Washington
Square Park about
Steinbeck
and Durell, went home and took bumps of coke while on the
toilet reading a beat to shit copy of
Penguin Poets
#5
(Corso, Ferlingheti, Ginsberg) and I started to feel
pretty, damned
good
about myself . . . (6 hours later) . . . something fun . . . in a bar,
with the blonde and a tall
hydro-geologist . . . she graduated high school with
2-dollar bottles from 4 till 7 and next thing I knew (with the
Garden State
Parkway whipping by) we were headed to Atlantic City and I
was slurring my words . . . brack jack-blacka jack, the blonde
riding passenger seat, hydro-geologist as driver, and I was in the
back snapping in and out of consciousness . . . on the boardwalk
. . . we each took 2 little pills to perk us up and 1 big pill to focus
our attention, I started to piss in the penny fountain at the Wild
West Casino and was dragged away by the scientist . . . saw a
nickelodeon and tossed a quarter at it but there was no slot for
change . . . ate a funnel cake . . . thought about black outs and

shaving my pubes . . . bracka jacka mister experiment . . . and by
the time we made Resorts, the uppers had kicked in and I was
starting to regain my edge . . .

Sat at a table, 15 dollar minimum, and lost 90 dollars . . .
The blonde was down 45 . . .
Scientist played roulette and was breaking even . . .
Cocktail waitress came by with casino dust and black hose
skimpy outfit wobbling high heel stilt act taking drink orders
wrinkled skin old tits leather nipples tucked into her waistband
and face creased with cocktail waitress desperation smiling . . .
Old Man overweight rose red patchwork crawled across his nose
in spider's arms veins and round old body shuffling moving
backwards away from the craps table cursing losing luck and the
slippage of American Dream . . .
Casino camera blinks its red light acknowledgment and camera
rolling camera recording vhs tape in back security room on
screen being watched by security guards with stun guns as the
Old Man shuffles backward like a diesel train in reverse and
Cocktail Waitress humps forward like tray balancing puppet act
and the two forces meet
train wreck crumbled puppet cut strings and the engineer asleep
at the wheel and
most importantly
the tray hits the ground in a slow motion movie about spilled
liquor and spilled chips . . .

"Never seen you move that fast before Johnny Boy!"
"I'm a man of speed, Mr. Experiment!"
"How much did you make out with?"
"25 and half a bottle of Yeng Ling, not bad."
"Not bad at all."

I got the blonde and the scientist and we headed out to the
boardwalk . . . I had the knob
off the arm
of a slot machine in my pocket . . . got in the car and smoked a
bowl, loose, headed away from bright lights and bounced checks,
cash for your gold stores, and excuses for the mortgage man . . .
gassed up, cigarettes, a bottle of water and a pack of gum, back
the way we came, I had my face pressed against the window

watching the sun rise with smoke floating out of my nose . . .
The scientist drove with a red-eyed determination funded by a 4-dollar pill . . .
The blonde played at deejay fidgeting turning dials and twirling hair . . .
The clouds rolled by in large white elephant formation . . .
The car hummed - The sun dripped - The clock read - The mind screamed:

"Closing Time Johnny Boy!"
(and I answered)
"Goodnight,
Mister
Experiment."


## Ꮽ GOOD LUCK, HALF HEART

flyby night in an easy town
there're eyes in the corridor, whispers of magnetic funerals,
draws metallic participants from across the globe, there're memories
of forbidden afternoons
and a high gloss escape out a second story window, memories of a young man
working on flowers and immortality,
half heart fed his resolve to the birds and kept the bread for himself, didn't understand
takes a certain amount of strength to play this game,
takes a certain amount of backbone that he just doesn't have,
young man wants to turn the plane around, runs up the aisle
only to realize that the cockpit's been locked,
and the pilot's gone missing,
realizes that he's just another passenger
and that all the passengers are scared, good luck
half heart,
you're gonna need it.

through subway tunnels
front doors
through tollbooths, past billboards
encountered 15 different cancers and split my eights down the
line

through pharmaceutical taste
red eyes
through 2 packs of Camels, up stairs
encountered 15 different cancers and doubled down on eleven

through old beer
puke taste
through smoking embers, at urinals
encountered 15 different cancers and stood still on twelve

through the state of New Jersey, across bridges, at rest stops
watching truckers and travelers and prostitutes - pulled into
Atlantic City round 4 that afternoon - ate at a dive of a buffet
where the service was foreign and the language unintelligible,
3.50 a beer and all this vicodin in my stomach, the food barely
edible, but cheap, filling when you could keep it down, and
memorizing the laws of winning, bringing down the house
advantage from 5.7 to .44, walking into Resorts on the
boardwalk and finding a 15 dollar table, changing 60 and
signaling the waitress, scotch-whiskey and watching the dealer,
hour later holding 240 and a good buzz, cashing in, the lobby
bar, guy that sat next to me at the card table materializes at the
door, nods hello and walks over, asking me how I did it, while I
sip on warm Dewars and chain smoke cigarettes, survivor of 15
different cancers, I can hear the cards singing from my seat at the
bar, shuffle sounds stronger than an orchestra, and I let him
know that insurance
is always a sucker bet . . .

Headed for the madhouse, the poorhouse, the sidewalk, a jail
cell, an early death, some sprawling three story on the west
coast, maybe overlooking the water, 2 cars in the garage, the
young drunken wife and a chain gang of children, sure, it's right
over the next horizon . . .

(Unexpected weight on my chest this morning, I felt I was
missing something; I had dropped something, forgotten
something - but what?
Turns out I wasn't breathing.
Life!
Life hid in my shirtfront pocket.
Bitch was disguised as a government issued check for 661
dollars and I had her by the throat. I had her by the throat with 2
inches to spare. I had her by the throat and that bird wouldn't be
singing for a while. I started breathing. Called in sick to work,
dressed and made it out the door.)

Headed for the bank, the unemployment line, the welfare office,
an early death, some awards ceremony for the Pulitzer prize,
dressed sharp in a 3 piece designer suit, monogrammed
handkerchief peeks out from the pocket, a gold watch, on a gold
chain, dangles real aristocratic like, sparkling and gleaming,
reflecting tiny bits of aristocratic light, sure, I can see it all now .
. .

(Dressed and made it out the door. Hit the street thinking about
problems; I've got tons of them - who doesn't?

Show me a man with no problems and I'll show you a man in a
coffin.
Life!
Life is all about dealing with problems.
A major problem is with self-importance. We all have an image
of ourselves that exceeds the concrete, an image that blasts us off
the sidewalk of the ordinary . . . upstairs,
we're all the next big thing, the next name up in lights, the next
icon to hit the stage. Shit! I cashed the check and bought an egg

sandwich. Ate the thing on a bench in the sun. It was about 60
degrees out.)


Headed for skid row, the free clinic, the rehab, a detention
center, an early death, some

small corner in the Lit section of your local bookstore signing
copies of my latest literal catastrophe, teenie bopping readers
with long hair and nose rings squirm and sweat, standing in line
with a scent coming off their crotches. I pat one on the ass and
smile, sure, can't see it any different . . .

(It was about 60 degrees and I was thinking flowers. Got off my
ass.
Took one train
to another train to a third and did a little walking. Wound up at
the Botanical Gardens.
Life!
Life was in bloom.
The rose bushes gave off an impression of underground
knowledge. They stayed rooted, stood rigid; it was as if they
were waiting for something that they knew was coming.
Meanwhile,
the wildflowers danced with indifference; disenchanted with the
globe,
they bent easy in the wind.
I thought the wildflowers were absolute madness.
I thought the wildflowers were absolute brilliance.
I had to ask myself:
How could they dance
and beam
with so much yellow
in the face of our future? And I had no answer. They weren't
talking and I couldn't talk for them and so screw it. I had 600
bucks and an unquenchable thirst.)

Headed for an early death . . .

(I had 600 bucks and an unquenchable thirst. Stepped into a local
bar and lost track of
Life!

Talked to a man
with a banker's nose and a shark grin. Gave the guy 60 bucks
and he gave me a square of tinfoil. I got into a stall of the men's
room.
Unfolded the tinfoil.
Thing held a pile of white rocks.
I began beating at the rocks,
pounding and hammering at them with the bottom of a BIC
lighter, breaking the rocks down into smaller rocks, into pebbles,
into gravel, into a silky fine
powder,
rolled a dollar bill tightly and sniiiiiiffffffft two giant lines for the
getaway, kick the heart into high gear as I speed off down Main
St.) I was
headed
somewhere . . . when I first started this thing
(seems like 20 years gone past) I had the illusion of goals,
objectives,
thought I saw a clear end (20 years
gone past) and after speeding off down Main St.
twitching, jumpy, heart pumping, arms jerking, legs kicking out
in wild Tango spasms, a
pink fleshy convulsion moving at a hundred
and 86
thousand
miles per second, I realized that there's no clear end to anything
round this place, there's only movement, one motion leading into
the next and rivers, tributaries, trickles into reservoirs, tap water,
urine, evaporation, rain runs down the side of a hill and flows
back seamlessly, moving so damned fast (me) that I outran my
body, lost definition and became milky white, translucent,
became an outline, grew vague around the edges and then I was
just a thought, just a whisper of consciousness blazing through
the mad chemical night . . . I was
headed
somewhere . . .

## ❧ IT DOESN'T GET ANY BETTER THAN THIS

there's nothing else like it
being young
and drunk
and wandering the streets of Manhattan
with a dollar fifty in your pocket

it's almost enough

another twenty five cents
and you can buy a large can of beer to soften the train ride home
and while walking along Hudson
you start to cough
and you spit something out
something brown
green
something speckled with red . . .
and lighting a cigarette, you sit down on the curb
and you study your handiwork
think
this is better than all the art that I've seen this year
maybe even in the last two years, but that's not true (last year
you were introduced
to a dead Russian in a motel room
a dead Russian with vision
a dead Russian who saw the future and trapped it with paint, and
you may have never found out his name,
but that doesn't matter) and getting up off that curb
cutting across Harrison to make the 1/9 uptown
you stick your finger in every pay phone that you pass
get lucky
find a dime
two nickels
a few scattered pennies

it's enough

you make Penn Station
and head for the beer vendor . . .

"Hello Mr. John!"

"Hey Ali, how's it going?"

"Very good today, very good. How are you Mr. John?"

"Ali, today, today I feel beautiful."

"Mr. John . . ."

"Yes Ali?"

"Today, you look beautiful, there is a light in your eyes." and he looks embarrassed, puts his head down and holds out the beer "Here Mr. John, no charge."

"Thank you Ali." dumping my change into the tip jar "Take care of yourself. I'll see you tomorrow."

and on the train ride home

reading Hemingway
Dostoevsky
Castaneda
Burroughs
sucking on a tall can of beer
watching the lights and the stores and the people zip by
you think to yourself
I hope it never changes
I hope it always stays this way
just being young
and drunk
and wandering the streets of Manhattan
with a dollar fifty in my pocket.


## CR HELL BOUND

In a bed,
on the floor,
at 7 a.m. in a dark room,
lines of
cocaine and a
semi-stiff
prick
I start thinking about my soul. (My father's got this real talent

for appraisal.
Man can strip your masks, disguises and tattoos, measure the
amount of steel in your backbone and the course of your intent
with a ten-minute conversation.)

In a bathroom,
in the shower,
7:10 in a dark place, fighting
for just one more
cocaine
drip
to numb the teeth and gums
I start worrying about my soul. (I've had these ten-minute
conversations with my father. Tons of them. And each time he
shakes his head, looks at me, and say's, like it's hurting him,
'With you, John, I just can't tell. It could go either way.')

In an alley,
in a car
that hasn't been paid off,
7:30 in a dark situation,
with cocaine
electricity
lighting up my thoughts
I start questioning my soul. (And still with that pained look on
his face my father will ask, "What do you really think, John? Do
you think that you're doing anything substantial? That when
your day comes to die you can do so without feeling cheated?
Or better yet, without being afraid of what's waiting up ahead?")

In a worn down body,
on a worn out street
7:50
a.m., with cocaine vision
directing my blood streaked eyes
I notice a speck of light
leaking in through all that dark. (Another talent that my father
has is gauging reactions. He watches the eyes, corners of the
mouth, takes note of the fingers and differences in breathing. He
can see the demon smile working its way through my body and
erupting from my lips. And with that pained look on his face, he

begins to walk away. My demon smile shines. I quote the words of a dead man. I start singing,

"I might be going to hell in a bucket, baby,
but at least I'm enjoying the ride . . .")


## ॐ IN DIRT

in dust
in bed at 3 am, there're stains on the walls
means someone's been bleeding, there's that pharmaceutical
taste
again
bloody gums
there's Faith
underfoot
and stray hairs on the pillow, the air conditioner drips
ice water on the comforter, and I'm soaked to the knees
in dirt
in dust
in bed at 4:30, there's shaky hands pouring drinks
means someone needs help,
there's that inflamed sinus wheezing
again
chalky nose
there's rehab
in the future
and an oddball concept of a tomorrow,
the phone rings from somewhere,
outside of myself, and I'm buried
in dirt
and in dust
and this 5 am bed scene,
an early morning death letter

Walking home from a bar I saw light in a window. It was
accompanied by music and the outline of bodies. I was out of my
head - always have been - and decided to check it out:

There was a man
and I didn't know the man
but he had wings, not the real thing of course, some light weight
plastic deal
strapped to his back.
Another guy wore a cat suit, leopard print, and was on all fours,
purring and growling, batting at ankles and rubbing up against
shins. One woman,
wrapped in a sheet of black latex, crotch-less by design,
swung a bullwhip while smoking
a long
cigarette.
Then there was a group of four,
acting
as a body of one (locked arms in legs, an elbow against a
shoulder blade, saw a toe against an ass, a nose in an armpit, a
solitary tit poked out of the jumble) and they moved collectively,
a rolling, writhing, sexual
mass
in the middle
of the floor. And then some glowing body ran by.
Glowing body was painted green/orange/yellow/red Day-Glo
swirls,
and I was slumped in a corner.
I was slumped in a corner and fiddling with an underage girl who
sported a neon blue hairpiece, a leather mini-skirt,
pierced nipples,
big knees, detached eyes and bruised,
purple
lips.

I was biting at her lips.

She moaned, pulled away, took a sip of whatever was in her glass (smelled like
kerosene) and spit something up from her stomach
(looked like blood)
then someone was yelling 'Lights Out! Lights Out!' and a rough hand grabbed me by the belt.
Rough hand had me bare and I connected the rough hand with the young girl and so that was all right; damned
blue hair pierced nipple was a turn-on. I reached out and found a neck, not sure who it belonged to,
kissed the thing. Glowing body reappeared. Ran by assaulting hell out of dilated pupils, then vanished.
Tricky fucker,
that body. Prompted me to smoke. Saw the business end of a cigarette dangling about 5 feet off the ground. Snatched it out of the air and put it into my face, took three drags and tossed it off into the dark.

"Here, drink this." Came out of the dark and there, I drank it. Automatically.
My mouth filled with saliva and I smelled something burning. Rough hand had me ready:
"This rabid
jumping cock, thing's
locked
in an erectile fit and
foaming
pre-ejaculate." Orgasm vibes came off my body like an odor. Cum junky came by and got fixed. Something was burning.
"Anybody else smell that?"
"Hey,
smell this."
A foreign wet softness jumped into my hand and I stuck a finger inside it. Heard a whiney noise. Felt sharp teeth clamp down on my arm. I retrieved my finger. Thing didn't smell too good.
"Here,
drink some more." If the lights were on I'd be seeing double. But the place was dark. My reflexes were quick and I took the thing in one gulp, gagged, and felt something stroking my ankles.
Something rubbed, massaged my ankles and finally pulled, hard,

I
went down, head met the floor and
'Lights Out!'

It was raining, no; I was only dreaming that it was raining. I was
in the dark, I was on my back, and I was soaking wet.
Someone was screaming, no; I was only dreaming that someone
was screaming. It was the sound of an alarm, random thought
flew by: "Anybody else smell that?"
I got up,
blind, disoriented, shit! Staggered, fell, crawled around, saw a
light and moved towards it. Light was a crack beneath a door.
Door opened onto a room. Room had a window and past the
window was a fire escape. John barely made it down.

At the bottom of the fire escape, and a little to the left, was the
cat-suited leopard man transformed into a biped. Next to him
stood the man with the wings. They were talking.

"This is fucking ridiculous. Try and have a good time and some
jackass has got to ruin it," said the winged man. "Shit, I caught
some guy fingering my dog!"
"No . . . Browny?" asked the cat-suited leopard man looking
shocked.
"Yeah."
"What'd you do?"
"Bit him. I didn't know what else to do."
"That's just sick. Who would try something like that?"
"Probably the same guy set fire to the curtains. You know what,
that's it, no more open house parties, from now on, it's invite
only."
"Honestly," replied the cat-suited leopard man, "too many
damned freaks in this city."

And I (John) agree,
too many damned freaks in this city; on the train, in the bars,
crowding the streets,
cunning hunter freaks set traps in public bathrooms and lead
young boys astray, holy roller freaks bring down pants and the
word of God, pain freaks step through the East village with
nipple clamps dangling and incense freaks scent the air while

drum freaks beat drums while horn freaks honk horns while
death freaks lie still while porn freaks buy porn while control
freaks control while news freaks read news while work freaks
work hard while escape freaks plan escape while poets write
poetry while I
sign this    -John


## ℂℛ INSIDE THE ACTOR'S STUDIO

She said something about the greatest tears
falling from the eyes of photographs . . .

And I whispered that the summer was close,
that we'd make it out alive . . .

She promised the impossible with a laugh,
and I told her that perseverance was the key.

She screamed
"The future has already been recorded!
What the hell can we ever hope to accomplish if we're trapped
inside of a photo?"

And I laughed
"It's only a matter of time.
One day, and soon, we'll get our hands around that damned
photographer's neck."

She sighs,
and says it's all a hoax,
that we're all being fooled, that there's no such thing as time
or forward momentum, that there's only screwing, just one body
screwing another body and that body screwing the next and so
on
down the line. Infinite ejaculate! We measure our progress in
orgasms,
and if it's a good screw,
well, then you're bound to come. Shit! Your history,
my history, all of history
is a hardcore pornography shoot. We're just bad actors

on a cheap set
and the director
has called in sick.

And I give her my best T.V. smile,
and grab her by the back of her neck,
and we hold that pose
as the cameras start to flash.


## ℘ I Need A Cocoon

I need a cocoon and four walls
plus bank-robber music
give me gun-shooting!
horse rider music! turned all the way up and words
a great rambling torrent of words
powerful enough to buy steaks with,
good steaks
steaks wrapped in bacon and
cold beer, barrels of cold beer
and a 5 gallon mug
to drink from
also a computer,
nothing special, just something to type on, oh, and some hand
lotion (gets lonely in a cocoon) and a razor, I MUST have a razor
in order to cut lines
from all the coke that'll be needed, and weed,
great bundles of green weed
with red/purple hairs as well as a pipe
or papers
and hash and a clothespin
and red rock opium
and black tar opium
and pills, downers, yellows, reds,
things that'll slow time down to a crawl so that I can REALLY
EXAMINE that bastard
and maybe figure out his secret.

I wouldn't mind a hammock, something to lie on that'll swing
me to sleep while in my candy empty cocoon
also cigarettes, boxes of cigarettes
to burn holes in my shirts with
to blacken my lungs with!
a bandana and a pirate accent!
a pencil and a sketch pad!
I prefer mescaline, but I'll take half an ounce of mushrooms or
maybe half a sheet of Jesus Christ
purple blotter
to bend space with, a copy of Scientific American
and a copy of Barely Legal
Shaved Asian
Teen Dreams, some Russians
Dostoevsky, Pushkin, Gogol
a few of the old Germans, a couple of Italians, 4 dead Americans
and this one A-
rab (can't remember his name right now) also give me a direct
line
to all the cemeteries of the world
so that I can ask Morrison,
Hendrix, Nowell and the rest (don't forget the uncountable,
unnamable
rest!) what happened?
if possible,
a lake, yeah, stocked with pike and trout
and large, pink and blind carp that I can fish for, catch, that'll
make me feel like I've got something over Nature and look at
John the provider, hunter-gatherer, skinner, scaler, filleter,
master of the elements in all his
candy coated
cocoon glory
and a miniature television set to watch cartoons, stand up
comics, and heavy-weight
boxing matches on
a catheter bag
so that I never have to worry about pissing on the floor
an insert-able rectal suction tube
so that I never have to worry about

wiping my ass
I'd also like finger puppets
I'll take 5 and name them, give them voices,
personalities, sexual relationships and
psychological problems that would be hashed out
in group sessions
and curbed with medications
I'd be playing the young doctor Dempsey role, so
I'll need a white lab coat
a stethoscope
a chart for taking notes
and a set of expensive glasses, also 5 baby coffins so we could
stage mock funerals
a tin of dirt and 5 baby headstones, I'll take a priest's outfit and a
handheld camera
to snap pictures of the young disciples with and, yes!, to
administer their last rites
a piano would help
also a piano playing guide so that I could learn to play something
sad
something slow and forlorn, something at 10:30 on a Wednesday
morning
something
about a cocoon.


## ❧ IT WAS IN A 45

dollar a night screw shack (place was full of hermaphrodites,
pimps, assassins and transients) somewhere
around upstate New York, sitting Indian style on a bed (thing
was a mess of fleas, mites, blood stains, lice crabs and dandruff
flakes) with the infamous blonde
and
we're half-drunk
off a case of cheap domestic (a mixed, processed, carbonated and
bottled golden liquid
fit only

for the palates of the most noble of rednecks and
backwoodsmen) playing cards
at 2 a.m.
and grateful
for our escape - we had beat the masses; the murderers, the
vampires, the electronic Japanese kids that crawl and buzz
through downtown Manhattan like robotic fruit flies with slicked
black hair - and their hair isn't even hair, it's ultra thin strands of
fiber optic wires and receptors and transmitters, recording sound
and image, recording taste, feel and smell, recording your
movements, my movements, your parent's movements,
recording taxi cabs and sex shops and book vendors, these wires
suck up every bit of that precious information and dump it all
into some central intelligence processing robotic fruit fly
decision making unit which comes up with theories, predictions,
classifications, calculations of speeds and distances, mapping out
plans of action and thought patterns, deducing trajectories,
orbits, ETA's and STD's then compiling, encrypting and
broadcasting indecipherable messages to some mother ship that's
hovering above Manhattan, maybe over by the Seaport
somewhere, yeah (area's a magnet for ET's,
ship jumpers, immigrants,
fruit flies and refugees) and we had beat them all,
started the car and moved North until the landscape became
snow capped mountains and small diners
by the side of the road, just a little getaway from the
concrete/steel/red brick lifestyle that we'd trapped ourselves into,
and retreating to this motel,
this little safe haven, somewhere
around upstate New York, enclosed
by 4 rented walls and the wolves kept at bay,
the silent phone,
a t.v. sits in the background,
we
dead bolted the door and stripped down to nothing,
took a bucket of ice
and beer
and hopped under the warm spray of the shower head . . .

it was in a 45
dollar a night screw shack, somewhere
around upstate New York . . . and it was perfect


## ∝ I've Called It Quits

taken a razor to significant junctions
while lying in the bathtub
scene finds me sucking on a tailpipe, big metal cigar, the
narrator,
or maybe it's the voice of some god, yells "Cut!" asks me
"What's with all this phallic shit, Johnny boy? You're supposed
to be the hero! Heroes don't come on screen with all that pretend
cock in their mouth! Underlying homosexual tendency in all this.
Cock gobbling insinuations will be made! Now, let's take it from
the top. And no sailor shit this time."
I've called it quits
there's a man, knows an operation,
asks zero questions, guy stuffs my molars with a cyanide gas and
makes me feel like a double agent, gives me careful instructions
about eating and guides me out through a back door. I wind up in
an alley.
There's a smell, I see shapes and I know exactly where I am.
Shit.
New York City is a jumble of plastic,
a cluttered, grimy
non-organic
heap.
The people don't even walk around here, they move exclusively
by use of the Want apparatus. (There's a system to this, a
scientific methodology, the desire-action equation, the stronger
the desire (the Want) the more probable the action to acquire -
ladies
and gentle
fuckers
of the press, I give to you
the Want apparatus)

The people aren't even people around here, they are parts of a whole and some parts are needed while others are not. (The demand for certain parts is a continuously shifting cycle, hard to control, hard to predict, thing is as volatile as a cornered wolverine and bears twice as many teeth. Only one thing is certain. Change. Today the market may call for lesbian street comedians, tomorrow the demand may be for telepathic Japanese stripteasers. Who knows? Scene in the Bolsch Temp Agency: Smoky, crowded waiting room. Typists, gun shooters, masturbation artists, painters, encyclopedia salesmen, mason workers, librarians, lesbian street comics, dentists, pick-pockets, knife throwers, gardeners, even telepathic Japanese stripteasers are waiting.

Mr. Bolsch is in his office, studying charts and figures, clears his throat, holds down a button and comes on over the loud speaker. Mr. Bolsch: "Alright, all you cunt licking hee-haws can leave now. The demand's been met. In fact, all you other fuckers might as well clear on out. We only need the ..." but there's a knock on the door before he can finish. The telepathic Japanese stripteasers already know. They're telepathic.) Only in New York City,

the A- train,

F- train,

the 1/9 uptown, street vendors, prostitutes, policemen, dog walkers, a million killers on the street and not a real face in the crowd. Cold eyes, cold ground, even the buildings are cold (the new face of architecture is a shitty one; cold, gray, steel, shitty). It's cold

year-round, just the way it works. It's a perpetual control measure, been specifically designed to keep us locked up in our heads for an eternity. Wrapped in layers of wool, heavy socks, scarves and pull down hats - THERE'S NO WARMTH - makes it hard to move in this weather, makes it hard to survive, hard to just be ...

"The next breath isn't feasible Captain. We're going down! All hands on deck! Man the life rafts!"

... I disconnect my self, slip a small German handgun into the waistband of my pants and make my way towards one of the life rafts. There's a green body there, roots barely developed . . .

"Captain, this one's reserved for . . ."

"Out of my way asswipe."

"But you're the captain, aren't you going down with the ship?"

. . . I pull the German handgun and create two holes where there was once wasted space; I'm an artist, definitely. I hop on one of the life rafts and cut the ropes, set my back to the East and start rowing, I've called it quits.

## ℭ LEAVE ME ALONE, I'M A MATADOR

I'll never be able to
hit a baseball
run a football
fight a bull
well enough
to make it

but if I had my choice
I'd pick the bull
in fact
I'd be the best damned bullfighter to have ever stepped into the
ring
I'd be deadly hummingbird graceful precise
I'd spin so smoothly and
so close to the animal
that the spectators would never be able to tell
where the bull ended
and I began

and when I type out these lines
it's the same thing
dodging horns
cape work - leg work - positioning the blade
and if I make a mistake
I come away from the keyboard
stumble out of the room
clutching at my belly

but that rarely happens
not much room for error
when playing at this game

a poet comes from over the top
down and
through the shoulder blades
putting the bull away
easily


## ❧ MANHATTAN TRAVEL BROCHURE (FOR TRAVELERS, COMMUTERS, DREAMERS AND CITIZENS)

So many things you can't do in this city. Things you aren't allowed to do anymore. War on everything; that's what this should be called. The War on Everything. We've got the war on drugs, on guns, on terrorism. War on obesity, on violence, on drunk driving. New laws, regulations, rules going into effect and small paragraphs tacked to the back of environmental bills allow for higher taxes on the already heavily taxed. All efforts filtering back to the original 2 percent. Parking tickets, court fees, expired meters, sin tax, sin tax, yes, increased cost of living, oil by the barrel for so much on the dollar, warheads, defense systems, talking heads to press buttons, concoction keeps the top 2 percent afloat in designer diamond necklaces, yachts, hand stitched French suits, other things. Even television is part of the works. Top 2 broadcast nationwide. Worldwide! Pump big city magic dreams to perfectly contented hicks on the ranch. Turn happy housewives onto brand names, fall fashions, new appliances, electro-dildonic-self-pleasuring-screw-omatic hump machines; yes, wildly unaffordable necessities that have just been invented yet were never before needed. Buy! Buy! Come! Hurry! Leave small town closeness for ant farm micro life. Become stars, actors, power lunching investment bankers! Become papier-mâché dolls and stumble by the sickly pretty buildings! The place where everything and nothing come together. The birth of Zero! City. Street's full of inside-less outsiders and chest-less breast feeders. Street's full of a thousand sets of titties, a thousand pussies, a thousand asses, a thousand holes, all of them sweating, grimy, caked in big city shit dust mascara and dumb eyes and perfume. All of them origami, lifeless, just compliant paper and neat folds, summertime skirts showing bruised thighs and shaving scars. (But there's something about them, or maybe there's something about you, who knows, that makes you want to chase and subdue those bits of folded paper, makes you want to reshape them, tear bigger holes, make new folds, sprinkle with water and watch the lines smear like so much shit dust mascara on the face of some young Spanish girl riding the uptown A-train, 90 degrees with no a/c, middle of August, that smell . . .) There's something about this place, dark, pungent, strong enough to infiltrate your thought process and send you spiraling through downtown, uptown, across town with empty pockets, wet mouth, stiff dick. There's a rancid buzz, an old yogurt energy that charges and juices you up and lets you run mad among billboards and taxis and black incense bandits. There's urinal using cross dressers with 9-inch dicks and red nails. There's a society of hobos, loonies, disease stricken and poverty driven living beneath the subway and railroad tracks of New York. They live with the pigeons, rats, roaches, with each other. Underground society and no law and murder by train light that fucker sto' me campin knife! Red river hi-ho! Can't walk around well armed. Can't take the law into your own hands, above ground, that is. So what's left for the little lamb with mint jelly around the ears? What's left for the three-legged underdogs and blind prizefighters? So what's left for you? And that you can't answer. Inside you've become acclimated to all this external hustle. Time sense acceleration, life joy devaluation, blinking slowly into the void, a street corner in the West Village, all this concrete and platinum movement gets you tuned like a watch; little gear clicks, big hand slides, tick-tock, tick-tock, as you shuffle along with the mechanic crowd. Welcome to Manhattan.

## ◌ PIANO WHISKEY UPSTAIRS

tonight it's that bottle of SKY
and regardless that I'm drinking vodka
it's whiskey piano upstairs
the fingers smell like pussy
used condom by the bed
9:17 on a Wednesday
piano whiskey upstairs
the blonde's long gone
I'm sitting here with a mug
fucking quick shot artist
piano whiskey upstairs
words at the sky
and holes in my shirt
I look at my dick
dreaming of piano whiskey upstairs
thinking of Billy the Kid
thinking of Nina Simone
a shortsighted young fuck-up
piano whiskey upstairs
Kimono condoms and hand-jobs
Siberian huskies and pay checks
John fucking Dempsey
piano whiskey upstairs


## ◌ LET ME TELL YOU SOMETHING

let me tell you something I've figured out . . .

cocaine and poetry

they work along identical orbits
there's no wetting your whistle
there's no such thing as one line
you type same as you snort
and each of the two substances . . . irresistible -

(I receive an e-mail from a man living on a continent I've never been to and he lets me know,

"John, you're the closest thing to Bukowski I've ever read. Keep it up." And I don't like that; it's enough to send me into a frenzy of broken keyboard and cracked monitor, enough to send me to the phone to make a call and 15 minutes later a man in an expensive car pulls up and hits the lights.)

cocaine and poetry

they tilt on the same tricky axis
there's no guarantee
there's no stability
you gamble with every word same as with each bump and soon
you find yourself . . . lost

(I receive a gram from a man driving a car I'll never be able to afford and he lets me know, "John, this is the closest thing to pure I've ever had. It'll keep you up." And I don't like that; it's enough to send me towards the kitchen with a BIC lighter and a dollar bill, my nose open, 15 minutes later I work on restoring the computer because I've got THE IDEA! for THE POEM!)

cocaine and poetry

they're a single train on a single track
you buy the ticket
"All Aboard!"
and there's no turning around
there's no hopping off at the next stop
you take that high speed ride until the end
and by the time you reach whatever (final) destination
you'll have figured out
whether or not
it was worth it.

## ℞ ONE FOR THE ANALYSTS, ONE FOR THE EXAMINERS, ONE FOR THE SCRUTINIZERS AND PICK-APART ARTISTS

I've replaced the Combine with the Machine (Kesey)
swinging from the rafters (line's reminiscent of Burroughs)
smell of death on her neck like a perfume (Ernie screams
through the decades
"You fucking thief!")
metallic twilight
of night's
shiny steel neon glow (sends Kerouac into a frenzy)
the most charming of cunts, teased my balls with her tongue, I
emptied two pints down her throat and waltzed out onto Mercer
(Miller shakes his head)
that money chin line
from *The Reading* (Fitzgerald raises an eyebrow)
scotch-whiskey while tracing a rhinoceros in the cracks of my
ceiling (Hank
sneers,
guy's beneath six feet of dirt
and stronger than ever)
I borrowed the beat from another John (Frusciante in
Amsterdam)
the bouncing, rolling, floating on the barge dream with the
typewriter jumping, leaving indents on the table (hey Tommy!)
"It started at my feet. Sucking up the smoke and where my feet
once were I saw an empty space, my feet were in the smoke and
the smoke was in the seagull and I began to realize what was
happening. The smoke was coming off my legs now and the
seagull inhaled it and my legs disappeared, and then my thighs,
and then my torso,
and then my chest was gone
and I was only a head
covered in smoke
and then I was only the smoke
and then I was inside of the seagull . . ."

(in there I met Castaneda)
a long sleeve, collared shirt of double fold Egyptian cotton and a
pair of hand-crafted, box-toed shoes made from the softest,
chocolate brown leather in all of Italy
(a gift from Ian)
"I might be going to hell in a bucket baby . . . " (Garcia)
and
BIG CAPITAL LETTERS
WILL REMIND YOU (of McCullers)
take the whole jumbled mess,
toss in two grams of coke and a prescription of valium, codeine,
xanax, oxycontin, a couple of the yellow
714 mg
lemon drop
quaaludes,
a job in downtown Manhattan,
no concept of a tomorrow,
a canister of Dust-off,
a large bottle of Dewars and a cheap case of domestic,
some long blonde hair
to tie it all up . . . (and you've got a Dempsey poem, enjoy
fuckers)


## ⊗ PARTY OF ONE


Having invited an astronaut and a great villain
Having invited a dictator
and a dead poet
One balding
strangulation artist
And one starving
office typist
Having hung streamers, red balloons, a blow-up doll, and
shredded newspaper for confetti
Having cooked the Baron's favorite meal
And purchased 2 bottles
of the General's

preferred scotch
I sat down to a movie theater silence,
a thousand kisses,
and piano, piano, piano


## ⌘ SOME NIGHTS ON THE STREET

you'll think you recognize somebody,
an old friend from school, an ex-love, or something, and you watch
for that familiar
smile or gesture, that certain walk or laugh you've attached to that person,
and then you pass them, get a good look and realize
that its somebody else,
the face is different,
the eyes are different,
their step is all wrong,
their hair a different color,
and turning the corner you see the bar, a woman, a dog with a certain look
of four-legged intelligence,
and you become happy that it wasn't that old friend or ex-love you just passed,
happy for not being trapped into one of those catching up conversations
that poison the night . . . kid like yourself
is always better off alone


## ⌘ THAT MESS ON THE SIDEWALK

There's something warped, wrapped up in love
that allows a man
to hate his woman
and vice-versa, yelling, foaming like

mad dogs,
and hands reaching out
to strangle the young lover . . .

There's something twisted, intertwined with love
that drives cars over cliffs,
and trunk over hood, a tumbling eternity,
hands reaching across the seat
in search of the young lover . . .

There's something so crazy,
so intense,
something so wild and compelling, there's
something that throws knives at the young lover's heart, there's
something that tosses axes from across the room, there's
something that trips, stumbles, pushes and sends
the young lover off the balcony . . .

(screaming 5 flights of affection)

Watching the young lovers from a window, there's
something
so human
about it all.


## ❧ THE FAITHFUL VIEWER

(there's a man standing frozen and he's watching)

Sometimes I'll wake up in the morning
shower, dress for the job
and on my way out the door,
I'll stop by the mirror to check my disguise.
I'll look in the mirror
and I'll say to myself, you know, John, all the smart men are
already dead.
And the smartest,
have died by their own hands. And I'll stand frozen in the mirror.
Just watching,
watching

cigarettes

pull
back flips.
They jump out of a box,
little
Russian acrobats, turn twice in mid-air and
land soft on my lips.
A match twists free of its root, suicidal fucker
grinds its face against a strip of phosphorous.
Sets itself alight like some feverishly religious type and hops 5
feet off the ground.
There's a cloud of smoke, and I'll stand frozen in the mirror. Just
watching,
watching

bottles

turn
cartwheels through the air.
They work their way from the fridge, wriggling and rolling,
tumbling through space and
settling into my grip. Brad Nowell
leaps from a grave in Orange County. Guy appears on my
shoulder,
and sings in my ear, "drunk by noon but that's o.k.
you'll be president some day" then
disappears. There's a river of golden liquid. Moves vertically
from the mouth of the bottle
towards the mouth of the author, and I'll stand frozen in the
mirror. Just watching,
watching

time
dripping down the walls and getting swept
under the carpet.
Watching the future
come on like some supercharged locomotive (you see,
for me, everyday
is a split second of deadly, lethal and terrible
enlightenment,

like,
right before a head-on collision, for instance), watching
a woman
undressing by a window, the husband comes home, chases her
around the place with a
12 inch
ear of corn
and a small tube of lubricant. Watching it all, two stray dogs
trapped in the sticky net
of curbside orgasm, watching the sun
bleed streaks of neon and realizing
that I had never made it out the door,
that I had never made it to the job and I'll stay that way,
standing frozen in the mirror. Just
watching . . .


## ℭ THE FINEST OF INNER WORKINGS


there's nothing wrong with
wednesday night bumps'a coke, there's a bar like a gas station
and here's me like a car, there's nothing wrong with numb gums
shaky hands
sweating hard, talking to unknowns and some knowns, telling
stories, drifting off,
there's dark corners and cunt dreams,
there's dead doctors and kerouac,
there's nothing wrong with red eyes, blacking out, snapping
awake
beneath a tarp, behind the bar, dick out and pissing poems, under
the spotlight,
yelling, loud,
"I'm the greatest living author this side of the Mississippi!" and
big hands round the shoulder, bartender tosses me like a javelin
"You pissed all over the fucking kegs!" ripped jeans, scraped
knees, bloody palms, finding my feet and taking off, hysterical
fit in my stomach, laughter
bubbling out my mouth, there's nothing wrong with

misplacing the car, the keys, your wallet, stumbling home and
climbing in through the window, stripping down and falling into
the bed, a small room, nothing wrong
with losing your mind every now and then, nothing wrong with 4
a.m.
except for 630 alarm clocks
except for the rough thursday,
except for the morning commute,
the job, the boss, the phone, the bad stomach,
the sensitive eyes, the slow mind, the dry mouth, this poem, ah,
fuck it


## ℂℝ THE OTHER MORNING


there was two knocks,
loud, search warrant, police-issue black shoe knocks at my door
and I lay bloated,
sweating, wearing a pair of ripped shorts,
my head ringing, hung over, lying on a mattress
on the floor
in a dark room. "John?"
I made a noise,
the noise tried to sound like a word, "Whaaaaggghht?"
It barely came out,
damned
late night whiskey and cocaine whirlwind,
leaves me with this raspy throat cancer scratched voice,
sounds like I been chain smoking Marlboro Reds by the carton,
"I wanted to see if you were up for some breakfast. Maybe
IHOP." IHOP?
Breakfast?
Breakfast what? John what? Who's talking to me? Me? Who the
hell am I?
"Who's there?"
"Who's there? What's wrong with you?"
I decided to open my eyes.
With my eyes opened it was like a switch got flipped and my

nose was turned ON
"Holy shit,
what's that smell?"
Someone had sprayed the place with the scent of ashtrays, urine,
farts, mold spores, vomit and old meat,
my brother stood in the frame of the door with his head turned.
"I don't know man, but it can't be good for you,
open a fucking window or something, light incense, do
something about it." Everything was coming together now,
well, my identity anyway. I started sorting out the facts, birth
date/place/name, address, the rest, pushed a cigarette into my
face,
came up with a match from somewhere off the carpet,
"Now,
what's all this about IHOP?"
"Breakfast. Food. You know, pancakes, eggs, French toast. Hey,
what's that hanging off your neck?"
I couldn't take more than two drags, did that and tossed the butt
into a cup half-filled with something that looked like gravy -
wait a second, I thought: neck, my neck?
And my hand shot up. Fastest I've moved in months. Ticks!
Ticks! Fucking ticks must've found their way in here, probably
been gorging on my sweet virginal liquor blood all night! Lime
disease! Ticks!
Hopped up,
my hands running across my chest and neck, searching, looking,
seeking out the little vampiric fuckers that in case you haven't
figured out, I'm deathly afraid of. Came up empty handed,
bewildered, heart pumping and my brother grinning in the
doorway -
cock sucker found the whole scene amusing. "What in the hell's
so damned funny?"
"That necklace you're wearing. Where'd you get that thing?" I
hadn't even noticed.
In my search for the dreaded tick bastards I had discarded
anything that wasn't a tick. Including the black string that was
tied round my neck,
and the silver painted
piece of plastic that hung from it. I stopped and looked at the

thing - giggled my ass off. The plastic was in the shape of a
dollar sign and it stood out big and bright, rap star
MTV
music video cash
money
big and bright, glaring and hanging, pendulum-like
off my neck and I just giggled my ass off. "I have no idea man.
I've never seen this thing before . . ." Pulling on a pair of jeans,
"but I like your IHOP idea . . ." the Burroughs t-shirt that never
seems to get washed, "but first . . ." just worn in the rain and
dried over the heat vent, "what day is it?" unmatched socks and a
3 year old pair of boots, "Gotta make sure that I'm not working
today, you know,
dedicated little worker bee that I am." Brother's still grinning,
this is better than TV for him, "Man,
you're such a fuckup sometimes. Don't worry, it's Saturday."
And I think:
it's all so "Beautiful, you know, this cash money medallion
really seems to shine on me, I'm going to start wearing it from
now on. It's perfect! Hey, think you can spot me some
breakfast?"
"Yeah, yeah,
c'mon, lets get in there before the place gets mobbed." And we
were out the door,
and on the street, medallion against my chest,
bright sun
of mid-March,

I had a good feeling.


## CR THE GREAT MOVEMENT

It came to me while sitting on a barstool.
I was beaten.
Depressed. I was thinking like a corpse. (There's dirt in my
mouth

and formaldehyde in my veins.) Shit! That's what I was thinking about. Shit.

Man was born to shit
and die
and that's it. There's nothing else. (I hadn't taken a shit in 6 days and I was beginning to get worried. I had read somewhere about a guy blew up from shit retention. Stomach kept on getting bigger. Face, legs, arms bloated and one day he just burst. Splattered the room with shit, blood and guts.

Imagine dying in such style.

It's too much.)

I usually get like this,
around the fourth or fifth day. (Fucking binges will be the end of me.)
Powered by little or no sleep. Powered by Dewars and coke with a lime.
Powered by pills and cigarettes and powders. Powered by some obsessive,
destructive,
all encompassing, hilariously manic and suicidal force that is stored somewhere in that rotten mass of jelly I call brains. Shit!
I felt weak.
I felt as if I was going to crack under the pressure - any minute now.
Everything was working to kill me.
Death was in each breath. Each step. Each shit. Each everything! Shit!
Death waited around every corner just hoping for a man to slip up.
I was losing my grip.
I looked at the bartender. He looked like a sack of shit and bones. Nothing else.
You know what,
scratch the bones,
he was just a sack of shit. I looked into him.
Saw nothing special. The same old thoughts.
The same hopes.

Fucking guy was concerned with haircuts and due dates and billing cycles and child support, blowjobs, submarines, dog food, lifting weights, gonorrhea. Shit!

I opened my mouth and called out a drink order. (Death around every corner.

Man with a pitchfork waits smiling.

Shit and die.

No shit and die.

A rigged game.

There's dirt in my mouth.) Bartender puts a glass down in front of me and stands silent.

Just looking like a sack of shit.

I make the liquid disappear, think to myself,

John,

you're so fucking beautiful when you're drunk,

so damned philosophical and lovely and having reached that conclusion,

I get off the barstool and start heading home. It had hit.

I finally had to shit.


## C&R THE LOCUSTS ARE COMING

The phone rang.

I picked it up and the Giant was yelling, "The Locusts are coming!

You have to warn people!

You have to get away from here! Get in your car and head north! Head to where it's cold!"

"Locusts?"

"I don't have time to explain, just go! Warn anybody you can and leave! Hurry!"

"Hurry where?"

"Oh, shit . . . I can hear them! What about you? Can you hear them over there?"

"Hear what? It sounds like static. Probably just a bad connection."

"No - oh, god! Hurry! Hurry before . . . Blaaaarrrrrgh!" and the line went dead so I hung up the phone and opened a beer.

Switched on the television.
There was a newscast on, a reporter was telling people to go into hiding, "...basement or nearest fallout shelter. Take only the necessities," he then read off a list of necessities:
Water
Canned Food
First-aid supplies
A radio, and I thought,
what about the beer? What about cigarettes? What about pornography and oxycontin? Huh? What about weed? Huh? But he seemed to have forgotten all that; he just read something from the bible and
"...God bless us all,
the locusts are coming." I turned the thing off, figuring that it had finally happened. The world had finally snapped. The whole planet had cracked, flipped out, gone off the deep end and taken a permanent vacation forward all mail to the psyche ward to be censored before it reaches our dear patient. I opened another beer and sat down at the computer.

I typed a letter to Leon the editor,
and then I typed a poem to some woman in North Dakota. It was dirty,
the poem, not the letter, full of sexual innuendo and erotic descriptions, I even had a picture of myself, in a towel and sporting a hard-on which I attached. I sent the two emails, lit a smoke, and listened to a sound coming through my wall,
"Bissmelah alrahman il raheem, malek yowm it deen, eeyaka naboodo wah eeyaka nasta een, ihdina serrat il moostakeen..."
Karim, the Arab next door. I knocked twice on the wall.
"Hey man, what the hell you doing in there?"
"Praying." he says.
"Praying?"
"Yes, today is the Day of Judgment. I don't want to wind up in hell. You should be praying too."
"Nah, it's alright."
"It's not too late for you. Come over and I'll convert you, we can

pray together! Yes! We can enter paradise together! As brothers!"

"Uhmmm, maybe later on man, I've got some work to finish up."

"If you say so, but remember, Allah waits not."

"Alright, Allah, I'll keep that in mind."

"Bissmelah alrahman il raheem..." I opened another beer, stretched and looked out my window.

Looking out my window I saw a young man running.
He was waving his arms,
yelling, "Locusts! The locusts are coming!" and he looked absolutely mad. He looked so wonderfully and perfectly mad, so delightfully and flawlessly mad that he might have been a great poet, or a great painter. Guy looked like an artist and so I opened the window and called out to him, "Hey, what's the matter buddy, why don't you come up here and have a drink?" But he paid no attention,
he just kept on running and yelling, looking both beautiful and mad while peeking over his shoulder, running from some invisible enemy, tripping over his feet, falling, jumping back up, yelling "Shit! The locusts!" running further away, spectacular - made me wish I had a camera.

So I started thinking about cameras.
Wondering how much a good one would go for, nothing too fancy, just something capable. I knocked off the beer and got up for another, opened the fridge and grabbed a can of domestic, opened that while thinking about cameras, drank half in one shot and it tasted so damned good, so damned delicious and satisfying that it made me think about my future. This is what I thought, 'I'll never get anywhere like this, just drinking more and typing worse and my liver has got to be beat to all hell, the lungs are up next, cancer around the corner and herpes down the hall and I'll never get anywhere, shit, anywhere at all . . . (I finished the beer, feeling disgusted with myself, truly, totally, completely fucking disgusted, and I thought some more and finally I thought) . . . screw it, every man is a machine and every machine needs fuel!'
I started screaming at the beer can. "Fuel! That's all you are, just fuel for the machine! No more and no less. Just plain old fuel!

You got that? Huh?"

"Crunch-Crunch"

"What was that?"

"Crunch-Crunch, Crunch-Crunch." And the sun had disappeared, blotted out from the sky and replaced with "Crunch-Crunch, Crunch-Crunch." And then I heard screaming, no words, just screaming, might have been the Arab, maybe he had gotten to paradise and realized that it was a fraud, or maybe it was that mad artist who had run away earlier, or maybe it was the beer can, who knows? Who cares? Crunch-Crunch? My windows began to bulge in towards the room. Small grasshopper shapes crawled along the panes and the wood started to creak, Crunch-Crunch, and I had a few beers left so I opened them all at once, gulped one down, stuck a smoke into my face, and waited for the locusts.

## ℭℜ THE MUSICIAN

Up since 11
snorting Norcos and drinking beer.
Up since 11 snorting - I should be working on the novel,
I should be pressuring Leon the editor to get out the second collection,
I should be
snorting Norcos and drinking beer and saying screw it, let it take care of itself while I
play the keyboard like a piano, while the mind goes numb and the eyes slide shut,
screw it, I'm a sponsored man,
thanks to this keyboard and a good friend (I've been running 12 hrs like this, jumping between the guitar and the computer (looking at porn (you just have to)), opening veins. the whole bit, to post another . . . shit, I can't even call this poetry; it's a half a case of beer and a nose full of white
playing the keyboard like a piano) - I should be discussing chapbooks with Renee,
I should be submitting to an Indian anthology, I should be doing

any and every
thing
that deals with
snorting more Norcos
and drinking more beer and playing this keyboard
as if it were a piano.


## CR WE'VE RUN OUT

All the good ones are gone. Bugsy
caught it hanging around Beverly Hills.
and Dillinger
caught it while coming out of a theater.
Capone
wasted away in Palm Springs,
syphilitic, demented
and almost
lucky.


## CR THIS ONE TIME SHE ASKED ME

is it something on the outside (meaning them)
or in here (meaning us)
or is it something beyond all this (gesturing at everything in
sight,
meaning God
or philosophy
or maybe even Death)
that puts pressure (her conscience)
on your chest (in her head)
telling you to turn back (that she's almost there)
that your next step
would be your last?

there's a six pack of talls
tells me I'm on my way . . .

sitting on a Tuesday night
with my numb face
and my numb brain
sitting here typing,
I hear 3 knocks at my door . . . all black eyes
and the head screams yellow . . . the blonde pulls white demerol
tablets like some old west gunslinger (literally,
I see Billy the Kid emptying holsters,
fucking guy's shooting pharmaceuticals with long blonde hair
and black eyes) my teeth crunch down heavy,
satisfied grin directs my face (pause . . . for sexual interlude: legs
wrapped, snug fit, hand in a glove when she mounts, feels like
the brightest of summer sunshine,
but you know that it can't last) . . . I get like this,
every
now and then, become lost, confused
abstract, barely understandable and nauseous with the head
spinning, damned
keyboard flying up into my face, jumping between thoughts,
basically, not making any damned sense . . . coherency
has taken the Greyhound to Fort Lauderdale,
has left me with beer breath and pill mind, my numb face and my
numb brain, tomorrow, what? I'm screaming about the calendar -
no way that I can make it through the next set of hurdles - bills
and punch clocks, subways, railways, side walks and the
electronic Japanese kids that I'll tell you about later on, next one,
I promise, but for now,
it's just too damned much, man's gotta take a dive
every
now and again,
fall down the stairs or slippery floor worker's comp maybe a few
months on easy street with grocery allowance and conjugal
visits. Conjugal visits? Yeah, sweating dirty in a small room

and three meals a day, oh . . .
shit,

my dick jumps at the thought . . .

and maybe that's where I should end it - Why? Cause I'm not
even here anymore,
I've been typing on autopilot. I've set the cruise control to auto-
write. Auto-write? Yeah, it's a set of fingers dancing drunken
along the keyboard - I'm not even looking at the screen anymore,
it's the fingers that're in control now, they'll take care of all this
mess that I've created, they'll
give you the nice big-bang Gucci fireworks display on Fourth of
July hardcore porn money shot ending to all this, they'll give you
the
sweet kiss
good night . . .

## ❧ WIND VANE SPINS LIKE A COPTER'S WHIRLING BLADES

It's not as windy as I thought it'd be
with the news of Israeli
suicide bombers (they've got it all wrong,
they need to focus on automated alarm clock factories
instead of on bus depots)
and remembrance ceremonies
and the dream my girlfriend had the other night
of her friend (lost
2 years ago today) and in the dream
this friend was
a Siamese twin (odd)
and one half of the pair was mangled
(that's her description, she said that) limbs torn
and blood running
charred skin
mashed face
but the other half . . . radiant!

Alive! Shining and beaming
with more light
and more life
than she'd ever seen before . . . (I told her
that maybe

she should be comforted
by that,
but the tears came anyway)
and then I remembered
the night I had spent at the Pig & Whistle Bar downtown
drinking Dewars

and blacking out

then coming to
in a construction zone, with floodlights and workers yelling
chasing me along walkways
and past large lumbering equipment
and I had no idea where I was
until I saw the flags, wreathes, and all the rest
I was hauling ass across ground zero (plus I'm scared of ghosts)
and it was windy that night too
. . . today, I'm stuck on that Siamese twin dream
(hell of a symbolic thing) and wondering if maybe that's how it
really is,
all of us with two sides
one physical that can be burned like kindling,
crushed like an old car
and one side
made up of something else
something that blasts through the cosmos and infiltrates dreams
something to let those who remember you
know that you're still around . . . maybe that's the wind I was
expecting today
and looking down from the roof of my office building (I can see
clear down
to Wall Street) I catch sight of a young girl's skirt
lift high up around her waist, showing thighs and white cotton
and I know that somewhere in the cosmos
someone's other side is laughing.

# ❧ Boost Ratings! Generate Comments! And Gain Electronic Friends Through Online Literary Postings!

Before we get to the meat and bones of this thing I'd like to state that I do not consider myself an expert on literary Internet sites. Nor do I feel that I am a sociological expert. All I want to do is lay down some observations. You fuckers can take what you want from it, take nothing at all from it, or not even read it - your choice completely. O.k.
Lets start like this:

I've been writing, or attempting to write, for close to twenty years now. I've been posting these writes, or attempts at writing, for close to four years. I can say, with confidence, that I know more about posting than I do about writing. The little bit that I do know about writing won't help you and so I'll leave all that bullshit out of this one. ((Note: If you are interested in taking the John Dempsey at home writing course, only 39.95, email mrdempsey@hotmail.com for details.) O.k. you pricks, I know, back to it!) In the following text I will impart to you, degenerate reader, the *tricks* or *secrets* needed to boost ratings, generate comments and gain electronic friends through online literary postings.

I've come to know these *secrets* through intensive research and personal experience. Furthermore, I'd like to state that these *secrets* or *tricks* have been tested not only by myself, but also by dozens of terrible writers, and have produced favorable results for all.

Here are a few questions, and please, please be honest when answering:
Do you want high ratings?
Do you want comments stacked at the bottom of your piece praising your inadequate abilities?
Do you want electronic friends?

If you've answered yes to one or more of these questions then step right up and I'll show you rotten bastards just how it's done.

Here's a nice simple trick. I picked it up at this pink little poetry site, which proclaimed in big, bright blue letters: "Over 50 (bad) Poems Posted Daily!" (Note: I should also tell you that all the drivel placed between brackets is the intellectual property of the author and not to be confused with actual, copyrighted statements. The author is just giving you the facts as they are and the drivel is no more than jaded opinion.) Well, of those 50 poems a day, the ones which received the highest rankings, were, for the majority, the ones that employed the *Cry for help* technique. This is a two-part technique. The first part is the *Sympathy-grabbing* title. For example:

*I can't go on with Life anymore*
or
*I wish I could disappear*
or
*My mother is an alcoholic-junkie who beats me with wire hangers which she heats on the stove*

These titles, and others along the same line, are a sure fire way to attract attention to your work. This will bring every alcoholic-junkie mother, suicide case and manic-depressive on the site to your page. Most of them will be ready to flash tens across the board without even reading what it is that you've put down.

The second part of this technique is for those that may actually read your lines and try to understand or help you. This is the actual *Cry for help*. What is needed here are a few statements that will really bring the *Oh, my god! What a poor, poor soul the writer is* reaction from all those alcoholic-junkie mothers, suicide cases and manic-depressives. Here's an example:

*I don't want the world and*
*the world*
*doesn't want me, I only want to be alone*
*and*
*not think of how many times*
*I've been burned*

Get the picture? And this was only a soft example. You can get much, much more out of your fans and commentators with something like this:

*When I come home at night*
*my mother is on the couch, passed out*
*with the usual bottle*
*and the usual*
*stranger.*

*I walk on tiptoe*
*so as not to disturb her*
*because I'm afraid*
*of that hot wire hanger.*

And if you noticed, the second stanza takes meter and rhyme into consideration. When you mix the *Cry for help* with rhyme and meter you have a real winner on your hands. Give it a shot cocksucker!

Next I'd like to turn you on to a *secret* I picked up not from just one site in particular, but from every site which allows running commentary. This trick will bring you high ratings, tons of comments and will start you on your path to electronic friendship! Fantastic!

I call this the *Extended hand* technique and it is really quite simple. The way to execute the *Extended hand* is by commenting on every poem or story that you can come across. Now, I'm not telling you to read them, just comment on them. Start by creating a list of generic comments that would fit in well under any author's work. Here's an example:

Stock Comments
Great write!
I can really relate to this.
You have a true talent.
Your words ring true.
Wow…
Very nice :)
I understand.
Perfectly done!

You write with great golden balls!
Good job!

When creating your list you must remember one thing: never criticize the author's work, even if it's constructive criticism. They simply don't want that. They want five star ratings. They want comments. They want a large group of electronic friends to chat with when they are at home on a Thursday night with a pulsating hard-on and a blank screen. C'mon now. Would you want criticism? Would you want actual constructive comments that make you question your writing or doublethink your usage of the language? Of course you don't.

Create your list. Make it good. Distribute your comments all over the place. Place them on children's stories and fantasy poems about the magical woman of the mountains who tends goats and brings the rain. Don't waste your time reading them, just comment. And remember, the more that you comment on another author's work and praise their inabilities, the more they will comment on your work and praise your inabilities.
Now isn't that nice?

Another *secret* or *trick* is the *Deep loss of love* technique. This is similar to the *Cry for help* technique in that it too is comprised of two parts, as well as employs the *Sympathy-grabbing* title. But in this context you can't have the last day on earth type titles, you need something really heart wrenching to bring in the middle-aged women, divorcees and single mothers out there. Try some of these out and see if they work for you:

*The love of my life has gone far, far away*
or better yet
*How can I ever show you my heart?*
or even better than that
*My wife of 15 years has leukemia and our three children burned to death in a barn fire outside of Minnesota*

Do you think it matters if you've been married for fifteen years? Or if your wife, or even your girlfriend truly has leukemia? No! The answer is no, it doesn't matter. You could be chasing some broken-down prostitute with a bad case of the crabs and all you have to do is feed these teary eyed titles to all your beautiful, new, electronic friends and then sit back and enjoy the praise. Isn't that magnificent?

The second part of this technique is the *Blue note* ending. This is basically a one liner ending that leaves your electronic friends hitching in their chests. You have to dump all the plastic emotion you've got in your little artistic body into one all encompassing line at the bottom of your work. As before, I'll give some examples.

*Ever since you left I've had the deep douche blues*
or
*Oh baby, can't you see that you've torn me in half?*
or (and this is one of the best I've come across)
*I am nothing until I hear your voice in the morning, echoing through my body and spilling from my rectum*
*in a haze*
*of magical light.*

See how simple it is?

Now here's the last one, and I saved this one purposely for last since it is the most powerful of the *tricks* or *secrets* that I've so far divulged to you, my dear reader and new found, electronic friend. This is what I simply call *The sex title*. There are three levels to this. The first level is the *hint at* title. Here you don't actually use the word *sex* just hint at it. Here's an example:

*The way he touched me*

The second level uses the word *sex* in the title but does so in a gentle manner with no promise of pornographic verse, like so:

*Between love and sex*

Note that the example given not only pushes the second level of *The sex title* but also grabs all the suckers for love who will read, rate and comment on anything, which mentions the word *love*. Now for the third level of this technique, this is where you not only use the word *sex* in your title, but also promise the reader an erotic interlude.

*Hot and horny, sexual Mary*

See - aren't you interested in Mary? Don't you want to know why she's so hot and horny? Don't you want to know what she's going to do about it? Of course you do, everybody does, we are all turned on by sex, and the allure of a stranger's sexuality will be too much for your electronic friends to turn down.

O.k. you fuckers, now you know how to reach the heights you've always dreamt about. You are now armed with the *secrets* used by some of the most highly rated, greatly commented upon, and well liked of electronic authors.
Happy posting!

## ℂℛ JOHN AS SAMSON

my weakness
is in the next breath
is in the next word that I type
or
in the next word that you read

my weakness is on the street
between legs
over my shoulder
everyone's the police
everyone's the gunman
the soft stepping enemy
the old women smiling

my weakness is the job
of pretending to be a spring or a button or a light bulb or a door
handle
on a Honda

my weakness is
end-of-the-month
anticipation
in answering the phone
in a voice
that my own mother wouldn't recognize

fed up with my weakness
with writing about it
living with it
petting and stroking at it like a tit

I decide to hell with the poem (for now). I walk away from this
thing. I get outside and start moving. I've got direction.
Intention. A game plan, sure. 20 minutes from here is a
neighborhood known as Alphabet City. I get there. The scene:
Newspapers on the street, coffee cups, empty dime bags, candy
wrappers, plastic bags like tumbleweeds in a ghost town.
Middle-aged Mexicans riding ten speed bicycles, wearing flannel
shirts with gold chains and gold teeth sparkling and reflecting as
they whir past ringing their bells, yelling "Chica!" Groups of
young tough black dudes in leather coats, on cell phones,
hanging around the ATM machines, whistling at cars and
smoking menthols. A few burnt out hippie kids with dreadlocks
and empty eyes and minds gone, sucked out to sea by some past
acid wave, and myself, heading for a building with flaky blue
paint. I push through a black iron gate that whines about the air
and the rain, that damned chemical mixture, and finger a button
marked 5-22; a buzzer buzzes, admits me, I climb the 5 flights,
knock twice, the sounds of a deadbolt being drawn back,
tumblers tumbling, clicking, the door swings open, arrival - my
last 20 dollars is always negotiable.
5 minutes later I'm outside packing a one-hitter painted to look
like a cigarette. I light up and suck down as much of the sweet
tasting smoke as my lungs can carry. Hold - Hold - Hold till I'm
choking, coughing and spitting, eyes tearing on the street and,
alright,
a calm flare runs up and down, all through my
mind.
Back the way I came, moving easier, a little lighter, side stepping
around potholes, leaning left, right, ducking under trees and
cutting in between cars without a thought - zero hesitation - a
sinewy confidence in my body, all the gray and pink parts and
pieces working in synch, in tune, hormones, endorphins,
chemical-electrical impulses and everything communicating with
one another and reaction, reaction, reaction . . . (Caught up in my
body and it's

internal
mechanisms,
I found myself on W4th, crossing 6th Avenue; I was between
Cornelia and Jones Street.)

Fantastic, I had walked about 7 blocks past my office and was
standing in front of a display window that caught my eye.
*Birthday Suit* I counted 3 mannequins in the window and
automatically assigned names to them.
The roll call: (from left to right) Red Leather Crotch-less
Holding Whip, Black Mask and Tassels with Zipper Mouth, and
bringing up the rear, literally, was Doggy-style in Blue Thong
and Clear Plastic High Heels. I walked right in.
More mannequins, half mannequins, torsos, chests, long nipples
pointing and lubricants, colored, flavored, in erotic shaped tubes
and jars plus dildos, black double-headed dildos that ran for 12
inches with a big jumpy vein and a fine circumcision line,
details, details, flesh colored foam-rubber cunts infused with
synthetic hairs and scented, perforated, slitted and clitted, just
right and ready for scratching that especially hot itch, there were
hangers of mesh thongs, vinyl thongs, sheer thongs with
butterflies and candy canes stitched into the crotch and also a
love seat, a metal and plastic affair dangling from the ceiling
with leg straps and a back rest, arm holds, an orgasmic swing set
for adults, French ticklers and vibrating panties that came with a
remote control, a chubby redhead behind the counter wearing a
tight shirt that was cut low enough to show a set of white capped
mountains . . . and I was thinking avalanche.
Her face wasn't half-bad, cute with big eyes and a big mouth and
I had a feeling that if I hung around for a little while one of those
big white tits would jump out of her shirt.

"Hi, is there anything I can help you with?"
"Yeah, I'm looking for Kimonos."
"Like a Japanese costume, to wear?"
"Yes, well, no, Kimono condoms, not costumes, but they are
Japanese."
"Yeah, we have those, they're right over here."

She also had this large ass that I checked out while she was bent
over fiddling in one of the display cases. The waistband of her

panties, baby blue, was visible for a second before she straightened up, holding 4 boxes of the Japanese condoms. She arranged them on the counter and I thought that the golden moment was approaching. At any second that albino tit was going to leap out of her shirt and I would snatch it up in my mouth.

"We have 4 different kinds. Lubricated, spermicidaly lubricated, non-lubricated, -"
(That tit! It was edging out of her shirt! Almost to the pink!)
"- and also a new one that just came out, -"
(I started opening my mouth. I was like a track star at the starting line. Exposing that nipple would've been the same as firing a starter pistol.)
"- these are spermicidaly lubricated and have Sensi-dots which will give her, -"
(She looked me over while I let my tongue slip over my lips.)
"- or him, added pleasure."
(Soon! Any second now I'd have all that glorious, milky tit in my . . . and then my thoughts took on a completely different track.)
"What did you just say?"
"That the Sensi-dots will give your partner added pleasure."
"No, no, no, you said her or him, I heard you. What? Do I look gay or something?"
(I was wearing a black crew-neck sweater, khaki pants, brown shoes; my work clothes, and if they made a soda that tasted like pussy I'd drink it by the caseload.)
"No, I wasn't implying anything. I was just being politically - "
"Politically nothing, while I'm here waiting for your tits to pop out, you're over there thinking I'm gay. What, did I say something that made you think I was gay?"
"What was that about my tits?"
"Or are these condoms only for gay guys or something?"
"No these are normal condoms that - "
"Because if you think I'm gay
I'll hop over this counter and - "
"I really think that you need to leave the - "
"- shove half my lower body up your - "

"That's it!"
"- chubby little -"
 "I'm calling the police!"
"- twat!"

I headed back up W4th, 7 blocks, occasionally smoking from the one-hitter and without the Japanese condoms. The episode in *Birthday Suit* had left me pissed off, annoyed at myself, getting offended by the chubby redhead showed a flaw in my character. I thought about it for a while and then said screw it; I'll worry about it later. If I ever find myself making a living on my knees, well, I'll have solved a mystery.

Not having any money, stoned, I eventually got back to the office and turned on the monitor to my computer. The beginning of a poem. It read:

my weakness
is in the next breath
is in the next word that I type
or
in the next word that you read

      And to that I'm now forced to add:

my strength
is in refusing the next breath
is in taking the next word that I type

and
making it the next word that you read

      Then there's:

my weakness is on the street
between legs
over my shoulder
everyone's the police
everyone's the gunman
the soft stepping enemy
the old women smiling

      Counter:

my strength is on the street
dreaming of legs
draped over my shoulders
everyone's breathing heavy
everyone's in need of warmth
the soft curving thighs
the young girls
giggling

And:

my weakness is the job
of pretending to be a spring or a button or a light bulb or a door
handle
on a Honda

I reply:

my strength is the job
of pretending to be a poet or a lover or a maniac or an artist
hanging
in a gallery

Also this:

my weakness is
end-of-the-month
anticipation
in answering the phone
in a voice
that my own mother wouldn't recognize

For the defense:

my strength is
end-of-the-month
anticipation
in making phone calls
in a voice
that any of my drug dealers would recognize

And finally:

fed up with my weakness
with writing about it

living with it
petting and stroking at it like a tit

    My answer:

to never be stopped by my weakness
I write about it
live with it
I pet and stroke at it like a tit
on some chubby redhead
working in a sex shop
about 7 blocks from my office

## ℭ FOR NO ONE IN PARTICULAR

"That's the last trap I'd ever fall into," he said
before knowing of
stronger animals
losing themselves
to soft hands

(this is for no one in particular

young husband
dreaming
of inflexible legs
and in the shower
with the soap
washing away
frustration)

"No way I'd be confined
and locked into a frigid woman." before realizing
he had been caught
tricked and tied
since the beginning

(this is for no one in particular

young husband
used to laugh

at the man in Penn station
dancing a slow time waltz
with a mannequin attached to his waist
to slow time music
while staring with slow time eyes
at the finely painted face
of his synthetic
dance partner)

"I'd let her know right off the bat,
no way for us to make it
if she can't attend to my needs." before fully
understanding
the definition
of necessity

(this is for no one in particular

young husband would think
poor guy, can't get a real woman
while waiting for the train
that would bring him home
to his own
special doll)

"I don't know what to do!
She's got me tight around the chest and I haven't been screwed
in months!
I haven't brushed up against a tit, or even patted her ass!
I haven't had a finger inside my loved one in what feels like
forever!
Oh,
how in the hell did I wind up here? How in the hell can I be so
crazy for a girl that just stares at my mouth when I speak, that
lays like a corpse, that doesn't make a sound while I squirm and
drown between her legs, that doesn't allow a muscle to twitch
while I'm begging for help?"

(this is for no one in particular

the young husband
doesn't

really get it
but I think that all four of them (the young husband, his wife, the
slow time man
and his lover)
should get together for dinner
and a movie)


## ⌘ CONVERSATIONS WITH . . .


I should be at home typing poems
instead of standing out here
in 10 inches of snow
at 4 o'clock in the morning
I'm on pills, I've been smoking weed, and
too many
cigarettes, (you eventually reach a point where
you want all of your footsteps to be poetry) and beer cans, beer
cans, I count 16
empties, there's
also
half a bottle of Dewar's in the kitchen and the lime's (you want
to shoot
guns with both hands - barrels at the gods(!) - until you reek of
black powder
and the sky's) been sliced up
hours ago in the kitchen
by the blonde and she's excited to be out here (dripping blood
across white snow and in each drop there's a line) away from the
telephone and the television
and the wood burning stove
giving us good
old-fashioned (good enough to make the dead
sit up and applause
your) heat, while the thermometer reads
5 notches
below freezing
and from inside comes yelling

and out here I'm shivering, dreaming that everyone's drunk on
(talent-
less ramblings, if there's enough dead, enough applause,
then you'll wind up believing and kid,) life,
while I mumble in the cold
to a man that isn't there (that's the absolute last thing)
in Stratton,
Vermont (that you want to do)


## C&R CORPORATE RECEPTION

Hello to small time souls
concerned with moving small time boulders!

(I keep one half at the table
nodding and speaking when it's needed
while the other half's at the bar, swimming the Mediterranean,
being thrown
from sky
scrapers.)

Hello to papier-mâché dreamers
dreaming newspaper machete dreams!

(Like confetti at a parade or
acid
rain

"Confetti of acid rain" . . . what a sight,
what a sight.)

Hello to bottom line feeders
sucking their way up glass walls!

(people who've never existed, or maybe they're holograms,
robots. I've never touched or smelled
anybody in a parade - how could I think different?)

Hello to practical thought promoters
rationalizing the necessity of a noose!

(But that's just the way I like to see things,
not smoke, but fire, and lots of it too. I believe that you should
walk around as if you're a piece of Southern
California . . . what a truth,
what a truth. I'm yelling)

Hello to white-shirted executioners
eyeing my neck with professional anticipation!

(and screaming,

"Let that body swing
once the gallows are built, for now
I'm content
just typing
my way
into these
little coffins.")


## ৫৪ ANOTHER MATCH


with cuts on my hands
the room was too smoky
*There're scars I'll never show you,*
*you'd have to catch me naked.*

with ashes on the bed
and a mirror on the ceiling
*Better than television or ice cream,*
*all this self-reflection.*

with the dream
of another match
of semi-death
and the small kiss . . .

Matchbook

and the thermometer
struck negative 12
in New York

with rings on the dresser
and hair in the drain
*A proper destiny for an ant,*
*chasing after the queen.*

with her running from the bathroom (the dream of another
match) wrapped in hotel linen (of semi-death and the small kiss)
I lifted the blankets high (yelling "Matchbook!
Matchbook!")
and the mercury rose with a bobbing
(scent of sulphur, a small flame) and all of a sudden
(yelling "Matchbook!")
it was 90 degrees
in New York.


## CR NOVEMBER'S LAST HURRAH

hung-over
under
a sun wailing -

poetry doesn't matter

under
a sun blaring
and screaming
to be heard from the sky -

even laughter doesn't matter

under the weight of November's
slowly
dying day
the nights are
slowly
killing you . . .

the hotel rooms are painted in pastel
pink, blue and yellow
with splashes of mirror

along the ceiling
behind the bed
across the walls
and no heat
and no warm water
and those special
Spring colors
at 55
dollars a night
like
Easter
decorations
like a time bomb
like a cancer
like a large
retracting vice
tearing you
and your woman
slowly
apart -

poetry doesn't matter

that morning
Sunday stood large
our eyes hung uneasy
and our souls
vulnerable


## ❧ NOT BEING A LEOPARD

or a hummingbird
or even a small
white moth
gnawing at an old suit
hanging
in your closet
I decide that

in my
next life
I'd like to be a helicopter
or an elevator cable
or maybe even a vase
being wiped clean by a housewife -
I figure that anything with a heartbeat
is faced with too many
challenges
too many
responsibilities
and it seems that every single one of them
is designed
specifically
to stop
that beat

but back to that vase
now that might be a nice gig
just water and flowers and housewives to bathe you
your own special place at the center of the table
learn to avoid the clumsy hands and
you'll have it
made

now that's something
I think I could be happy with


## ❧ NEW YEAR MECHANICS

I sat down knowing it was whiskey
there was Johnny Cash in my head
telling me about the big river
and I had spent a lot of time
sleeping on bathroom tiles.

December was outside
showing pale hips and ass
and something inside of me yelled

*A sky-full of late nights!*
And then I was thinking cocaine
while putting my money on the bar.
*The Curse of Time!* yelled the calendar.
*This year is going the way of everything else!*

More history for the printers
and soon I'll be the self-proclaimed Black-Out King
of two thousand three.
Where does it all go?

("Spin back the reel," yells some Thing, somewhere, "let's watch
that last year in
fast-forward."
"Yes sir!" answers the cosmic apprentice.
"Shake up the deja-vu scene a bit."
"Understandable sir.")

It goes the way of everything else
down the tubes
down the page
down my throat
in a fine spiral
and at midnight
we dig our way
out of a 12
month hole . . .

*I ask that we observe a moment of silence.* While standing
graveside
I see fireworks
and that line
seems very
familiar.

# ❧ THE GREATEST PLACE TO DROWN (FOR LISA)

Always that time when you were moving, not exactly dancing, more of a
vertical writhing, a charmed cobra movement of your body, and David Bowie was in the background
telling us
about modern love . . .

Always that time when I kidnapped you from the ketamine party (after
drinking with Reilly for 6 hours in a college bar, it
seemed the most reasonable thing in the world) and we rolled parked cars
out of the driveway and into the road,
and I grabbed your keys
and forced you into the back seat . . .

Always that time in a New Orleans hotel, off the plane less than 6 hours
and you were puking in the toilet while I was puking in the sink, the smeared mascara,
we held onto the counter to keep from falling, but
that didn't work, there was years and smiles, certain photographs,
things
beyond our understanding . . .

All these times (I've discovered a method to convert moments to water!)

liquid -

that runs into an open drain,
is fed through special pipes that transport eyes and memories, pipes that transport
the wildest of 2 a.m. promises . . . and so if I ever ask you to go swimming,
but

it's the middle of winter
and you don't see a pool,
just
think about the picture
that hangs by your bed.


## ℭℛ STREET SIGNS MURMUR


mumble, whisper like
they want me to spend the night in jail

One Way, Stop, Reduced Speed Zone
Ahead
but that doesn't stand for much
in the face of all this beer, I've had to swallow my own puke
twice tonight and it's only
2 thirty in the morning in
the black pickup truck with
my mind somewhere
else

"Perry Farrel on repeat! A thousand times porpoise head!"

while reaching for a match
striking a light and burning my fingers,
swerving for the small kiss
the tiny death
the sidewalk under my tires and my mind
somewhere else

"John Frusciante guitar! A thousand times murderers!"

as red and blue
electric eyes
wink excitement and reflect
watch dog passion and zero
tolerance law for the state, it hits me
that I may have
left my wallet at the bar

# ❧ REFERENCE GUIDE

I was nothing
I am nothing
I will be nothing
from this point forward
not a photograph
or a postcard
not even an old song
playing on the jukebox in your favorite bar


# ❧ SOMETHING 3 HANDED

There's man, wrestling with shadows
wondering about footsteps
echoes and busy signals
red traffic lights
from subway to train to cab to the graveyard
from school to office to bank to the graveyard
from amoeba
from ape
to man to the graveyard to 4 years old
and worrying over skeletons

"From down here I can see it all!"
(and he's talking worms
booby trapped tunnels and old wooden cabinets
he's talking something 3 handed
with the greatest
of poker faces)

There's man struggling with corners
gears
shadows
he unhinges and something
3 handed
springs open

"There's immortality down here!"
(but I'm not so sure I believe it)
"There's answers and warmth!" (and that's a lie as well)
"There's sights unimaginable and cunts unheard of!"
(I almost fall for that one)

from one night to womb to light to the graveyard
from dancehall to wedding to hospital
to the graveyard
from apples
from worms
to man to the graveyard to 65 years old
and growing thin around the edges

"What's there to lose?" (and he's talking card games
long sleeved dress shirts
and overconfident to a point that
gives me a feeling the game's rigged)

"Dreams fulfilled!" (but I start to think about it)
"Greener grasses!" (and that's what I've been looking for)
"Easy legs and
70 degree winters!" (I reach for my wallet)

"See that,
nothing to be afraid of. Just a little gambling! No more bets
folks! (but I'm the only one standing here) No more bets!" (and
he's talking something 3 handed
with the greatest
of poker faces)


# ◌ WITH HER PACING BY THE ENTRANCE


It's crazy
beyond
comprehension, a vision, I'm left unsure

I've done something
committed to something
I've got one extra death to worry about now

one extra
hole to fill
one more wake to attend
and I need to figure out
something
heroic
to be inscribed on the tombstone

soon a big gong will sound
and a Dead End sign will flash
and I'll be cold on the floor
of a Men's room in Nevada


## CR WEDNESDAY NIGHT I WAS

drunk enough to stumble, drop bottles, and tell the bartender
to fuck off when she reminded me
that my change was on the bar, and for the second time in my
life
I noticed a 6-inch Mexican (dripping wet and looking pissed off)
crawling out of the toilet
and pointing a small revolver in my direction, but I was standing
at the urinal,
counting piss bubbles,
examining my dick,
wrapped up,
when I heard a tiny explosion,
and my legs gave out (the floor's
tiled with sheet metal,
(an attractive offer) I'm John the
ridiculously
magnetic animal) and then I heard the Mexican laughing
(sounded real evil and it echoed)
as he ducked back into the toilet
and everything grew dark

# ❧ THE RED LIGHT OPERA

The red light opera
frightens and confuses me
maddens and depresses me
comes down like winter in a Russian novel
or like a prize fighter
hit with
a hard left.

The red light opera
sends me running to hide in the bathroom
forces me to sit naked on the toilet pondering my legs
and dick
and kneecaps
and fingers
and if I had a small mirror
I'd examine my asshole
as well.

The red light opera . . .

I get off the train and head towards the parking garage. I pack a
bowl, light up, cough, and start the car. I get onto the street.
Honk the horn. I've been drinking beer on the train and I make
the mistake of getting in line with the rest of humanity. I see
their faces. Watch their eyes staring out through the windshield.
Not a flicker;
no soul,
no guts,
no heart,
nothing, I was surrounded by tennis rackets, by wireless phones,
by old pencils and dog collars, that's it. Just objects without
dreams, or maybe just the dreams handed down to them by their
manufacturers, but not me, I was special; I had real dreams. For
instance,
I was dreaming of 20 tabs of oxycontin, 20 tabs of vicodin and
20 sticks of xanax. I was also dreaming of a 12-year-old bottle of
Dewar's Special Blend that I saw a commercial for on late night

television. I had pangs of want, wild spasms of want, I had traveled 20 feet in 10 minutes and it seemed as if I might explode from the want before I could do anything about it. There was a sea of red lights and a pressure in my stomach like gas. A strange noise came from my belly button and I farted. All that want. I was almost positive that I would explode in the next minute or so. I would take out an entire block with the force of my want explosion. I would destroy schools and cemeteries and ice cream trucks with it. The light switched to green and a thousand objects - suicide musicians - flung themselves into the body of traffic. I moved another 10 feet, applied the brake, and listened to a thousand horns bleating out their red light opera. I lit a cigarette. All that want in my stomach and lungs and brain. All that opera pounding at my ears. A bus came barreling through the intersection and added it's deep bass contribution. I was hunched over the steering wheel with ashes falling into my lap. All that want stored up inside of me, all those dreams, and with my luck, there would be a car crash or a power outage, a police sting and they would pinch the body-building Iranian I buy pills from, there would be a fire at the liquor store destroying their inventory of scotch-whiskey, or maybe a flat tire that would force me off the road. But I couldn't think about that, just the goal, all that chemical and liquid and both of them as good as an abandoned gold mine or a purse found in a parking lot for a kid like me. I brought my foot down on the gas pedal a second before the light turned green. Shot in between a gray moving van and a motor scooter. Made it under a yellow light. Past a strip-mall. A sharp right, all that want, I was going to make it, and then a dead stop. The orchestra was warmed up. They played a dream-crushing concerto and flashed their red light awareness. Someone in the audience, enthralled with the music, cursed and gestured with his hands, made fists, pointed a finger and howled. I was nervous. The opera crowd was growing shifty and I didn't trust them to begin with. I couldn't understand their tennis racket reasoning, their dog collar lives, I didn't want to understand, all I cared about was satisfying my want and I started to get worried that it wouldn't happen; their metallic fatality statistics, their combustible gas minds, all my want and a wall of red lights blocking my path, I grew beyond nervous; I

became scared. I pulled into the shoulder with my heart
twitching, saw an opening and punched down on the gas . . .

I shot around the horn section and the drummer,
blew past the stringed instruments,
powered by fear and want and loud revving dream engine,
powered by smoke and chemical
aspirations,
I left the tall red light conductor
sputtering green
in the wake of my exhaust . . .

The red light opera
sickens and pushes me
revolts and compels me
forces me to react like a salmon
like a buffalo
like a getaway driver in some old movie
about a bank heist gone bad
with the sirens crashing
and the sirens screaming
all in time
with the rest of the band.

## ೞ THESE THINGS ARE MY BIRTHRIGHT . . .

Astrologically speaking,
I study my Glow In The Dark Stars (both dippers, Orion, and
Cassio-
peia)
on a ceiling that tells me (late at night, in an accent
laced with cobwebs and cracked paint)
that I just
may be
ahead
of my time . . . but
I'm smarter than that,
understand that it's an attempt

to throw me off guard - stupid ceiling
doesn't know
(crash and bury all you want) that I've been training for the
ambulance,
I've been running laps around the emergency room,
I've been jumping from rooftops
clutching at an umbrella
and building up my tolerance
to ricin
to strychnine (Strychnos nux vomica and
Castor
beans) - There's
proof!
There's 3 bottles in front of me
but I'm already fucked up, seeing everything in duplicate,
triplicate, quadrupli… (my woman's got
4 heads, 8 nipples,
I've got
12 hands and
1 hundred
plus fingers! Breathing's
rather shallow . . .) There's
more liquid, but I need cigarettes.
And ever since the clock's
been busted
there's allot of extra
time
hanging around.


## ⌘ LETTER TO MATT MILLER
## OF AUTHOR'S DEN

Mr. Miller - just finished reading through your email - I
appreciate the follow up and the opportunity you've extended to
help me become a sponsored author. I've spent enough time
posting/preaching/ranting/bitching/making connections and
reading over at AD not to respond.

First time I logged on and saw the following business slogans *Membership fees* and *Upgrades!*, *Grace periods!*, the rest, I wanted to punch a hole through the screen.

9.95 will never buy you, or anybody else, a year of art. How could it? 9.95 can't even ensure the quality of that so-called art since there isn't a criterion process. Cleared checks, validated credit card numbers, money orders and Pay-Pal accounts don't force the words to line up.

On the other hand, 9.95 might buy you a notebook, a pen, if you're lucky, 2 six-packs of Blue Ribbon beer and then say you come home to an empty place and you sit down on some lawn chair/milk crate/stepladder, rip open that notebook, slug 2 beers right off the bat, and scrawl every inch of your guts across the paper - Imagine that! 9.95! And let's just say that you're a man with only the required amount of guts to operate around this place. You've got the bare minimum opening the door for you. Let's say you've got about 3 sentences worth of lit rolling across that notebook, 3 damned sentences! It'll still be the best-damned 9.95 you'll have ever spent.

Matt, Mr. Miller, founding father and President, my intentions are all within the bounds of the "Spirit of Author's Den." I'm not writing this to rip into you, criticize you, I'm not writing this to be some talent lacking jack off that needs a place to post his work, I'm just writing this to be honest- business?

I understand business. I've always been good with numbers - 9.95, 24.95, I understand that it takes money to maintain a place like AD, but you could charge a penny a post and it still wouldn't be the right thing - the only thing a writer/painter/musician/sculptor/axe juggler/snake charmer, quasi-artist of any arrangement should pay with is TIME. You take all the TIME that should be spent pursuing family and friendships, financial securities, paying off mortgages, working at some job, hanging yourself in a motel room over a restless woman and her tennis instructor, all the TIME you spend laughing over picnics and standing in line at the bank, the TIME used to fit in, to shape/mold/twist and contort in order to pop out of some finishing school cocoon, a finely functioning cog in that mad hat machine of the Stock-Fucken-Life, all that goddamned TIME! Sweat! All that blood! Damned nights you can't sleep, in front of a computer beating at a set of keys until your hands are cramped, vision comes in duplicate, triplicate, quadruple fold print and still, you look that fucker - TIME! - in the eye and you let him know, *I'll pay my tab when I'm ready. I'm not ready yet. I've got more in me. Lot's more.* And its not that 9.95 that'll allow me to push on, its just this little sack of guts hanging round behind my stomach. That's the only thing I need.

Matt - I like this place - it brings out allot of different characters; half hearts, halfwits, full wits, even some damned dandy commercial creators that can sell cartons of autographed, rhythmic and rhyming poems, but you know what's even better than all that, it brings out the 3 meal a week, the lone desperado type that's got no 9.95, that collects vices like trading cards and carries one hell of a set of guns. If I get sponsored, shit, that's the muse, or the gods, or just plain literary luck - if not, well, good luck on the business.

- John

## CR GLASS

of dewars and 7 beers
the cards working against me . . .

I lose 40 to the blonde
and think about strangling her, 20
to the kid that
thinks he's leonardo di caprio, I'd
punch him in the throat
without thinking twice
then
15 to the girl that looks like a guy wearing a skater's hat, I'll
reach across this table and knock his
hers
whoever's
teeth . . . bad moves

I'm full of them
bad ideas
I've got nothing else
I wind up in a 93 volkswagon
with a hundred and forty
thousand miles on the engine
driving around in 2 inches of snow
waiting on something to change


## ❧ A 10 Year Old Conversation
## With The Giant

Holy shit!

I told you it was good.

Yeah, but (I grab at my nose and lips, pinch both cheeks)
it's like I can feel everything up here (pointing a finger at my
temple). More than everything . . . Everything magnified!
Everything amplified and blaring and everything under a
microscope! While the rest of me is numb (I slap myself across
the face to show him what I mean).

Ha ha. You're crazy man.

(He's crazy, damned Giant. We were 17. In his parent's house
with no idea about reoccurring patterns, Chaos theory,
Determinism, the blueprint of tomorrow, unavoidable futures, as
if we had signed up for a dance class without realizing we'd be
learning how to dance.)

So this guy and his two daughters picked me up today (I lived
about 2 miles away and used to hitchhike). It got me thinking.

About what?

That one day I'll probably have a couple of kids.

Who isn't?

Let me finish.

One day I'll probably have a couple of kids, and even though I've always thought that I'd want a boy, it might not be so bad having a girl.

I don't know man, all that tampon and ovary talk, forget it. I'd much rather have a boy. They're tougher and you can teach them all kinds of stuff, shit, they could be anything, pirates or Vikings or vampires or something. Bounty hunters!

Honestly!

Or ace fighter pilots or ninjas! What are you going to do with a girl?

Well, I'd give her a hell of a name.

Oh yeah?

Yeah, that's what I've been thinking about. The guy that picked me up today, you know what his daughters were called?

What?

Mary and Christine.

And?

Well, it's so common. I wouldn't call my daughter something like that. I don't want a little Jacky or Betty running around the house. I'd call her Cocaine!

Ha ha. You're really fucking crazy.

No, I'm serious. Just think about it. You can say things like, hello my baby Cocaine, my pretty little shining baby girl, and it would be alright. In the mornings you can play with her and tell her, oh Cocaine, I've been thinking about you ever since I went to bed last night, dreaming of you, just itching and waiting to be with you again.

I don't think you're allowed to do things like that.

It would be fantastic! She'd be pale as a ghost and stay up all night asking questions. She'd have no regard for a clock or the sunrise. She'd chew her fingernails and talk real fast. She'd be beautiful!

There's something wrong with you.

So beautiful that I'd run away with her and we'd go live in the mountains somewhere. We'd get married when she hit 18 and start a family of our own!

You're sick!

And maybe we'd have a baby girl and name her Cocaine as well. She'd be even more beautiful, twice as pale and talk twice as fast and stay up twice as late and so tuned up that she wouldn't even believe in Time!

Man, I don't want to hear any of this (he was focusing on a 5-inch square of mirror and a razor blade). You're a fucked up person.

Maybe, but I don't think so (I was fingering a tightly rolled dollar bill).

Whatever. Here man, you ready for another one?

Oh my precious and darling Cocaine!

Shut up already.

My delicious little sweetheart!

You crazy bastard.

(We were 17. In his parent's house with no idea of how close we were to a truth. We snorted another bump, and started talking about something else.)


## &#x03A9; A 20 Line Lesson

listens to Jimmy Buffet

thinks I need to be more of a pirate

and she's right
in a way

it's in the living, in the actions of NOW - that's what allows you
to fill a page
a man can't write what he don't see
can't communicate what he doesn't know
playing at reporter is one thing
but playing at god is another
creation,
yes
a vivid imagination,
sure
but reality . . . true connoisseurs can tell a fake from the first line,
will smell the plaster used for the cast and denounce the
reprinted Monet
carbon copyists are Xerox machines
the great impersonators are lumberjacks
what's needed is a razor blade
and a strong set of shoes, a writer's gotta climb that metallic
divide
and dance a mighty fine line


# From *Steps To The Madhouse*

## CR 3 Verses, 4 Emails And Some Other Shit

and there's a million boys in the Midwest
writing lines
twice as epic
as mine will ever be

there's also an Asian in the corner of some coffee shop
and I can see the Pulitzer Prize winning words
dancing
behind his glazed eyes

I sit here in front of a screen
reading mail

John - love your style, just wanted to say hello.

John - what are you doing? Why do you keep writing such
horrible poetry?

John - I know where you live, enjoy dodging bullets!

Fantastic-
one idiot
with a bottle
holed up
in a dark apartment
with the ability to type
a few
weak verses
is actually being read - Fantastic!

Another letter reads:

I am a vigilante seeking and destroying John Dempsey
imposters I find via
Google.com, since an incident in Manhattan brought me
face-to-face with some
Irish sop claiming the name. And make no mistake,
blather-boy: I have
chunks of guys like you in my stool. I am the genuine
article, you're a
copy of a copy, and I'm the
copy shredder.

JOHN DEMPSEY!

Well -
it's a step up
from eviction letters and past due bills
and I've been itching to have my ass kicked
for a few weeks now,
and my hands aren't all that small - hell
I boxed The Lost Battalion Hall for 3 years - light on my feet and
sticking

the jab to tough guys in Queens - Hell
I've even knocked out a movie star

(at a casino in St. Martin, they were shooting Speed 2 and this
one's all mouth and curly hair, he's ordering drinks just as fast as
I am, we sit across from each other at the card table, he's got an
actor's pass dangling round his neck, making all the wrong
moves, I've been on Dewars since 7 this morning and now I'm
down 300 bucks because of his card play, Mother! And he keeps
eyeing me, making remarks to the waitress that I can barely hear,
and it's
Action!
before my mind registers the intention, diving across the table,
knocking him out of his chair, straddling his chest and planting
the right hook to the chin, follow with a quick jab to finish up -
and he's out
Cold! . . . damned
actors
with their
glass
jaws)

Sorry - sorry, I completely went off there, lost my place in time
and wound up back on the Islands, o.k., back to it - (but, I don't
even know where I left off, I've misplaced my flow somewhere
around here and all I want to do is close this damned thing so
that I can make the bar down the block and, and . . . fuck it! This
idiot thing is finished.)


# ❧ GOOD ADVICE


it was maybe 7-8 years ago,
and I had yet
to read his work

face in the toilet
the night's liquid
pouring from my mouth, I was
sick,

the world a merry go round and an image
came to me - white beard and wild,
green dancing eyes

I didn't know who he was, I had never read his words or seen his
picture, didn't know his life or his art
but somewhere,
on some level, my
body cried

one of the Greats! one of the
few
true
Artists . . .
PAY ATTENTION!

and so when he told me

"from the gut
john,
do it from your
gut"

I
did


## ⌘ PEP TALK


and you figure that you'll feel all that much better if you force
the tears - you haven't cried since 1985 and that's a lot of shit to
have in your head - since 85 there's been more mind fucks than
you would have previously thought possible - the pretty girls
with their summer
goodbyes
and
pouting
lips,
the legs
that stretched
from a bedroom in New York to a hotel

in L.A.,
the fading friends
that can barely recognize
those eyes
you've been toting around and even the mirror
plays games (2 days ago you looked in that glass and saw a dead
man -
delusion bought 7 yrs bad luck, and if you last
that 7
then baby,
you'll have
surprised most . . .)


## ᴄ℞ THE EDGE OF FRIDAY MORNING


beer breath - cigarette shakes at fingertip's end - new pain in
ribs, second from the bottom, right side - left eye nervous twitch
- 4 crumbling teeth - dry soles - back muscle spasm - sleep
disorder - schizophrenia - bad credit - low morale - addictive
personality -
stained shirt - chapped lips - throat shit and equilibrium shot -
dry soul - chewed nails - delusional - 10 scars, right arm - 1
circular growth, inside, right elbow - 2 scars, forehead -
20 plus hospital visits, frequent flyer miles - black truck, bad
debt - 6 days,
waiting on this next paycheck - and 3
vicodin will
slow
down
time -

heat rash - weak ankle - 3rd metacarpal fractured - insane woman
- insane job -
insane poems - better than no woman, no job, no poems -
suspended license - application denied for a firearms carrier's
permit - rejection letter from the oyster boy review - 5 beers into
Thursday night snapped the high E, Fender acoustic - bitch -

middle of the neck, slipped disk - irregular heart rate - high
cholesterol - black lung - heavy liver - vomiting on her
tiled
kitchen
floor -

Europe and Asia - Mexico - Cairo -
Greece - the island of
St. Martin and the
Mediterranean sea, mad at second place, when you walked in the
door -

suicidal tendency - poor blood circulation - rotted nasal passage -
2 warrants in two states that I don't remember visiting - 20
cowboys smile on the range, welcoming me to their country,
admission: 5.25 -

take a razor and carve a cross on the inside of each arm -

they tell me that there shouldn't be any blood in my puke - they
tell me that smoking dog hairs will make me crazy -

check engine light - fuck - low gas and bad mileage -
my American dream:
3 tons of piss and rubble - middle aged oriental digs at his crotch
- and you can usually find me, 5 days a week, downtown C, 8:25
in the morning, and I'm usually
hung over -

read 4 books a week - play guitar - write shit - take shits - blow
snot - hearing in my right ear has become intermittent - the heart
that lays
in this
cruel
and
dead face - tossed her away, 40 million dollar father and all -
beach house in San Diego - gone - the works - said screw you
baby, I'm a man of movement, places and people and dates to
keep - guitar riffs to play for fuck's sake and you're in here with
the whining and marriage talk - and the piss
offa
your cunt - meanwhile,

I probably loved her - late night, long distance
phone calls to some woman I looked up in the phone book - and
32
alcoholic ounces
disappear
on a 10 minute train ride -

pimple on my cheek - 1 gray hair from watching the world trade
center collapse - picked a cigarette from a stranger's ear by
bumping him with my hip, his attention focused below the waist
and my fingers darted forward,
plucked the smoke,
retreated - frugality -

walked three blocks and came to an apartment building, rang the
buzzer for 4L - she bounced outa the place on fine summer legs,
all woman - eyes bleeding sunlight
and the city took a bow
as she turned in the wind -

the piers at South Street Seaport and the fish cleaners and the
waves - the salt air
dusted our skin -
11 a.m.
mahogany -
the Irish bartender - Mexican beer with a lime, snorting speed off
the urinal in the men's room,
I made up a poem - it was hot - damned hot! - but then I forgot it
while ordering the crab cake
special - 2 years later I jumped from an airplane - 1 year earlier I
jumped from a moving car and in high school me and this head
case named Tom would jump from moving trains, we would
land in the snow mounds created by snow plows - now I get
messages - messages from people on the internet - some guy
sends me rhyming death notices, a woman sends me dripping sex
words,
a website sends me an advertisement:
*The Hottest Teens on the Internet Love Their Pets* - oh
yeah . . . and if anybody is interested
in a men's
steel

Movado - this year's sport model, featuring the black, museum
dial, silver tone hands and Movado's
signature
concave dot - just email me - mrdempsey@hotmail.com - and
I'll give you a good deal -

next door the dogs bark and I think about feeding them aspirin -
outside the pigeons coo and I think about feeding them alka-
seltzer -
in my room I mix a 6 am drink and think about feeding myself
these quaaludes
(picked 'em up from this guy called Mr. 714) - and if this phone
rings just one more fucken time, and if the voice on the other end
is some type of fucken salesman, I swear to god
I'll burn this building to cinders - and, and . . . all this shit
keeps happening in my life - strange occurrences - my Visine
being replaced with liquid acid, waking up with thumbtacks
driven into my thumbs and a tattoo on my back (it says
something
in Japanese) or waking up in some town on the north shore or
DRING-DRING,
DRING-DRING - of that fucken phone! -

"HELLO!"
- silence -
"I SAID FUCKEN HELLO!"
- more silence -
about to hang up when I start to hear music -
a song - country,
rock
type

"My head hurts
My feet stink
And I don't love Jesus
This kind of morning
Must have been that kind of night
I keep tryin to tell myself
my
condition
is improving

And if I don't die by Thursday
I'll be roarin Friday night"

and the line goes dead - only in this city -
Jimmy Buffet - and my face was split in half by a smile - I
opened a new beer - drank a toast to the wisdom that had just
been conveyed to me, over the phone, by some unknown source
-
drank another to the sun, shining blindly, outside my New York
window - understood that it was Friday,
last night was Thursday and shit, I wasn't dead -
not that I know of - why,
I don't love jesus -
and my feet,
they smell like shit, wait, wait, yup my head hurts -
oh yeah, and my condition;
it was definitely improving.


## ℃ℛ I'D LIKE TO MAKE IT


I'd like to make it

On the stock market,
buying low
snorting till I'm . . . sorry, my mistake, I meant
selling high
insider tips on
corporate mergers
and the floor
alive
with 5-piece suits

I'd like to make it

At the tables,
of Vegas and the Caribbean
high stakes hands
leading to 100 bills
spread

across the mattress
as I throw off a drink
and slice
into lust fueled orgasm
with a cocktail
waitress

I'd like to make it

As a gun man
some
typah
old west shooting artist
pulling blue
*steel*
flash of barrel and cylinder as leather gives way -
bullets streak across the landscape with Matrix cinematography -
bank teller: "It's the Dempsey Gang!"
last words, spoken through bloody bubbles
jump -
to a sunset scene
4 cowboy types count gold coins
and talk with
drawling
killer accents

I'd like to make it

With a typer
putting out
original and
epic
scripts
instead of
paltry words
on subjects,
already dissected,
by better
(god damned hacks!)
scalpel men

I'd like to make it

With you
and your friend that works down at the bowling alley, maybe 3
a.m.
in a cheap hotel,
off the expressway

With the neighbor's wife
in her sheer little night gown,
showing long legs
and firm
*ass*
bending
for the morning paper

With

the young
Asian secretary
that I see on the morning train

*the middle-aged*
banking exec
with the sexy
orange glasses and high
heel shoes

With the Swedish blonde
at the supermarket down the block,
apron and all
pumping!
on the conveyor belt as customers
grab a cheap feel on their way out the door, and
one man pulls a camera from his coat pocket, begins to shoot . . .
the "Supermarket Fantasy" spread comes out a month later in
underground pornography shops around the city, I pick up two
copies - sign them as if I were some sorta artist
and realize -

that I'd like to make it
in any way
possible

meaningless

the 60 dollar phone bill
the past due rent
the screaming
woman

pointless

cell phones
don't soothe the soul buddy
rent
ain't gonna make the nightmares go away
and the screaming women - huh,
well you know what that's worth

"paycheck to paycheck"

measuring breathe
so that I won't suffocate before the 1st

"cradle to grave"

a 30 day life cycle

(timeline on the sidewalk)

automated teller machines
that tell me nothing -
automate me to nowhere -
leave me stranded -
picking half smoked butts from the gutter (such a dirty habit!)
fishing for anonymous drinks at the bar (such a horrid young
man!)
laughing,
at the 65 cents -
front left pocket -
that I'm trying
to buy the sun with

(conservation and sanity)

last night
I fought for an hour and a half
cursing
and twisting
a cap
from a bottle
of Listerine - and I think it's a good thing
that it wouldn't open

I was in rare form


## ℭ I THINK THE ANSWER IS NO


"John"

I live in No-Time
walk on No-Land
breathe in a blend of oxygen and despair - it comes off the
crowd, heavy and rancid
as I work my way
across the stage; the stage is New York
*City*
streets with Half-People shuffling
Dead-Steps
to a broken
dance beat

"John"

I sit in No-Space
crawl through the No-Plane
bleed a rotten mix of Dewars and hemoglobin - it pours dirty,
heavy and rancid
as I push my way
towards the edge; the edge is a fine blade
*slicing*
reality with a steady hand working
Dead-Fingers

to a broken
dance beat

"John!"

I love with No-Heart
say words with No-Meaning
dance a disgusted tango with...

"John, damnit - all I need is a yes or no answer here. If you don't
wanna go out just tell me. I don't need to hear all this."

"I thought I was telling you, just let me finish."

I think with No-Mind
see with No-Eyes
perceive a Dead-World...

"O.k. John, forget it, I don't want you to come out anymore. I've
already had enough of you."

"Look baby, I was just about to finish up my spiel, why don't
you hear me out."

"Last chance."

I pay with No-Cash
drink with No-Liver

. . . The line goes dead

I hang up the phone with
No-strength
take a sip from the
No-Bottle
and end this
No-Poem


## ✣ N.Y. Sex Pills


About 50 minutes ago I started taking these pills.
Now . . . I'm not talking the regular pills - not the
vicodin,

valium,

codeine

and xanax type pills, nope, not today. Today I'm on something
different. Instead of all that, I'm eating things like

Boom and

Horny

Goat Weed, African fly tincture, others - natural, herbal formulas
with

90-day,

money back!

guarantees. Things made from a blend of

five herbs

found only

in the mountains of Brazil.

(Now,

why am I doing this?) - sitting here, alone, watching triple x
films and beating hell out of myself. (Not sure) - but on a
Monday night, with a stomach full of beer

it just feels

like the right thing

to be doing - the CORRECT

thing to be doing.

On screen: a young Asian, back bent and mouth open - behind
her is this black dude and he's holding some sorta python - in
front is a white guy, pinching his nipples and holding a snake of
his own.

On the couch: me, jacking off and spilling beer into the cushions.
(Now,

why am I doing this?)

There's a weak explosion.

I hit STOP on the vcr and work a beer out of the cardboard box.
The cd player is on repeat and I must've heard this song 60 times
so far -

every time it ends I stare off into the corner, squint my eyes and
from the side of my mouth -

"Play it again Sam." - then I run over to the corner, lean against
the wall (now I'm Sam) -

"Again john? You've gotta be kidding me." - back to the couch

"Yeah Sam, just one more time." - again to the corner
"That's what you said the last time the song ended." - couch
"But I NEED it - just once more and I'm done, promise!"

the track rewinds and the Frusciante's *Murderers* plays for the
61st time. I scream "YES-YES!"
at the ceiling, take the volume up another notch and dance
around the place. There's a guitar amp in the middle of the room,
the cord stretches across the floor and as I execute the *fouetté en
tournant* my lead foot gets caught. I go down hard, teeth punch
through the skin of my upper lip, forehead meets the stained
carpet and there's a nasty
*THUD*

I don't spill a drop of the beer
but I see stars
for about 30 seconds
and in a detached,
clinical sorta sense
I notice:
I'm still hard. (Now,
why did I take all that shit? What am I gonna do with all this
dick sticking out in front of me?) I get to my feet.
Blood pours down my chin and I wipe it off on my sleeve. (I'll
tell you what I'm gonna do -
why sheeeet, I'm gonna WRITE GODDAMNIT!!)

"Captain, will you please power up The Machine." (in a refined
yachter's voice)
"Aye-aye john, (in a pirate's drawl) full system power in 5 – 4 –
3 –
2 . . ."

a new beer and I'm at *The Machine*, still hard, I type;

Women

that's what I want

women

women with long legs and soft
breasts

women with long hair and small
hands

women

what I don't want:

women, like the women
today

I don't want -
Corvette women
or 3 stories in Palm Springs type women
or silicone cherries
with heavy lipstick and
man made
noses -

I don't want Paris vacation women
shopping at fucken Tiffany's

I want real mouths and
real arms

I want
real eyes

- "horrible
shit!" I might as well type with my dick for what I'm producing.
I hit the POWER button, yell
"Mother!" and walk out of the place. I'm not gonna find any
women around here. Maybe they're all
downtown . . .

I take the A - 4 stops
and hit the *Slaughtered Lamb* - no dice, some raven or something
has already been through here, has taken the eyes that I'm
looking for and gobbled them up for himself -
"MOTHER!"
I make the *Village Idiot*, *Barney Mac's*, *Live Bait*,
*Hogs* and (FUCKEN) *Heiffers* - nothing,
nowhere - "MOTHER!"
I'm running around the city,
ridiculous hard-on flapping against my thigh, my lip is still

bleeding and I haven't seen a pair of
REAL
eyes
for blocks - BLOCKS!

Screw it!
back on the A, back up 4 stops, up the stairs and through the
door (I'm like a bad movie
running backwards on the projection reel) - I never turned off the
cd player and *Murderers* blasts through the apartment, 3 beers
left of the twelve and I'm still hard - Fantastic! I start calling
phone numbers:
1-900- HOTSLUTS,
1-900-ASSPARTY - I ask a female voice what kind of music she
likes.
Has she ever been to new york?
Favorite author? -
NOTHING
That's what I get -
NOTHING,
and guess where I'm going - NOWHERE
at light speed, (STILL HARD) down to the last beer, (STILL
HARD) the last sip!
and then I hear it,
it comes through the walls on wet sound waves, reaches my ears
with a hot force and claws at my libido.
The scene takes on the quality of an 80's skin flick - it's the
woman next door - moaning loud - headboard pounding with
wild rhythm;
Aye - Oh-
Papi! (THUD-THUD)
Oh - Ahh (THUD) - 1 voice, (Oooh - Conche!)
she's alone, (Hyeeee!)
and she's HOT! (THUD)
Maybe as hot as I am! (Uh!)

(Hey -
wanna see me move real fast?) BANG! And I'm off the line,
tearing at cabinets and searching under the bed, finding half a
bottle of wine, a few loose condoms, grabbing the sex pills,

wiping my lip one last time and jumping out the door. I run
down the hall, KNOCK-KNOCK on her door - "Look, I can hear
you from my place. The sound is making me crazy - driving me
nuts!" she answers with a flushed face, wearing a bathrobe - I
bring up the wine, point down towards my belly and her (REAL)
(I'm slowing down)
eyes (slow)
follow - we both smile.

We chewed the sex pills, knocked off the wine, smoked no-frills
cigarettes and woke up in the morning to *Murderers* still
pumping out of my stereo.
I was hung over; red eyed and on the verge of puking - walked
over to my apartment, turned off the cd player and asked myself
- "Now john,
do you really think
that doing this kinda shit
is gonna get you anywhere?" - no answer, I was busy -
on the phone -
"Yeah - yeah, I need the same thing tonight. Give me the Boom
pills and
the Horny Goat Weed and a bunch of that African fly shit.
I'll be in around 5."


## ◖◗ FROM THE NEW GRAFFITI DAYS
## (WITH SPECIAL THANKS TO RENEE)


I have been busting ass and beating keys to get the words down
on the page - I
just need to get the
blonde
offa my lap
the white coats
outta my living room (and I would've thrown in those
fucken
pigeons but I took care of 'em yesterday, 2 a.m. - bottle
rockets and dewars w/coke, one rocket veered off

course (a slight
miscalculation
in wind speed and lift) - the body builder in 7g is
screaming for a replacement "Hey - you have any idea
what that window costs? If you don't pay up I'm gonna
take that money out of your ass! I can hear you laughing in
there!
Open this
fucking door!") - I hit the fire escape, 15 bucks in my pocket
and make the downtown bar -

downtown bar: sitting with The Giant (he's a 6 foot 11
370
pound
Lithuanian) we drink draft beer and smoke killer
cigarettes -

Giant: hey - you know who got out yesterday?
John: who?
Giant: Wingtips, that's who.
John: who the fuck is that?
Giant: you know, Kenny, the Kenny you've been fighting since
high school.

(yeah, I know Kenny alright, we've been going at it for years,
bar-room brawls and back alley showdowns,
shit,
guy almost ran me down in his Ford Bronco one night.)

Giant: well we call him Wingtips now. remember, he got pulled
over and tried running away in a pair of wingtip shoes.
John: shit, I thought he was away for another year or so.
Giant: nope, walked yesterday, you know he's gonna come after
you again.
John: think so?
Giant: yeah, definitely, he's been away 2 years, lifting weight,
pounding ass - probably been thinking about you the whole time.
John: fuck . . . well, let him come, that kid's always been small
time; I've handled him before.
Giant: yeah - BEFORE - that's the operative word here john, by
now Wingtips is 200 pounds! all muscle! probably one of the

toughest bull queers upstate - you better watch your ass.
John: you may be right, he could be on his way here right now,
heading straight for my ass! MY ASS!
Giant: you should get yourself something, something serious,
like maybe a pearl-handled magnum.
John: I don't know man.
Giant: well, think about it, I just happen to have one at home,
and as luck turns out, I'm looking to get rid of the thing.
John: oh yeah, well what do you want for it?
Giant: shit, not much, give me a buck 75 and its yours

- so now I'm looking to make a buck 75, the body builder from
7g is looking for a new window, the blonde has gotten off my lap
(now she's throwing dishes around the apartment), the white
coats have grabbed their nets and hopped back into their truck,
they blast euro-trash techno music and speed away (I've been
hiding -
in the closet w/a mannequin - (4 hours now)
she's the quiet conversationalist) plus
Kenny Wingtips is coming for my ass -
MY ASS!
but there will,
I repeat; There WILL
be something
to show
for all of this - promise -
dempsey honor
and all


## ଓ THE BLOCKED COLUMN


There have been 15 attempts to write this column. 15 scenes of
lifestyle have been typed, read and then thrown out in disgust.
SHIT! The deadline was flying at me. The deadline carried
literary brass knuckles that would knock me into drug binge and
depression if I couldn't meet it. Never before had this happened.
SHIT! I typed 10 poems a week. I had the storyline for 8 novels

at any given time. SHIT! Just waking up in this city, breathing in that gray, New York air would get my mind buzzing. The words would string themselves together as I went through the routine of being alive. All the subway hustles and freakish night streets, all the lunatic blondes and tough characters had provided me with hundreds of lines. HUNDREDS! But now, I had nothing. Not a creative
drop.

It was weighing me down.
I had to
DO
something.

So,
I broke my own drinking records. I caused bad scenes of yelling and violence. No dice.
I took pills and smoked long joints till coherence was a thing of the past. No dice.

Then,
I realized: a fresh start! That's what I needed. A clean slab of rock that I could chisel away at until it mirrored the image in my thoughts. If I could just dump all the past writes, make all the old words disappear as if they never existed, then, maybe then, I would be able to write.

I launched myself at the task.

Step 1: ID the ghosts.
By ghosts I mean all those horrid pieces lying around my apartment, all those
past writes and
old words.

Step 2: Capture the ghosts.
I filled a garbage bag with everything I had written. Hundreds of poems and essays, even the beginning of a novel where these strange German doctors, leftovers from the days of the S.S., were 3 feet tall and wore black latex suits. Every time the techno version of *Walking on the Moon* was played, a dark station wagon, resembling the old ambulances of the 50's, would pull up

in a screech of tires, the doors would fly open and these little German doctors would hop from the car. They carried scalpels and when they moved, it was with a camera trick speed. As they closed in on their prey they would smile and their teeth were needle sharp points - pure shit, all of it. I gathered every scrap of paper that held my words, every bar napkin, wrapper and notebook, every drawing, sketch and/or outline, and tossed it all in the bag.

Step 3: Exorcise the ghosts.
I took the hibachi grill, used for the summertime roof top barbeques, placed it in the center of the room and filled it with the ghost papers. Looking down on them I was filled with a sense of finality. Seeing all those words and understanding the blood that had gone into writing them, the crazy nights that I had survived and then later documented, the exotic drugs and insane women, all that lifestyle, all that sweat and I was going to shut the door on it, the point of no return, a terminator line,
so to speak and I lit a match,
took the flame to a corner of one of the pages and
crossed over.

The papers caught, every one of them was on fire and they burned brilliantly.

I added more to the pile, pulling them from the garbage bag and placing them in the flames. Soon I had emptied the bag, but I saw that the flames were still hungry; I began tearing apart cardboard boxes and tossing the pieces into the fire. I started chanting: more ghosts, more ghosts. Then I burned my garbage, newspapers and milk cartons, old letters and bank statements, everything, and still, it wasn't enough (more ghosts, more ghosts). I broke up a wooden chair, and after the first piece caught fire, I knew I was in trouble; there was a lacquer of some sort on it, my apartment filled with a nasty, acrid smoke. I stopped chanting (no more ghosts, no more ghosts). I ran for the kitchen and came back with a pitcher of water. The smoke was heavy and as I dumped the water into the hibachi there was a knock at the door, SHIT! I tore it open, gagging and teary-eyed.

(Intro The Neighbor)

"Hey, what the hell is goin on in there? Where's all that smoke comin from?"

"What smoke? I don't see any damn smoke."

"Look wiseass, this hallway is filled with smoke and it's comin from your apartment. If it doesn't stop in the next five minutes I'm calling the police!"

"O.k., o.k, no problem, look, we don't need any cops here. I was just lighting some candles is all, I'll put them out now and air the place out. How's that?"

"Just do it! And fast!"

I closed the door and checked out the scene; the smoke was still thick so I opened the window and let all the smog and airborne scum of Manhattan into my apartment. After about 15 minutes the place was pretty well cleared out and I was feeling good. I had gotten rid of the ghosts and now I sat in front of *The Machine*. I was celebrating with a beer and psyching myself up; time to get the words down, fantastic words, serious, spellbinding words, words that would capture the reader and leave them begging for more, another line, another stanza, another
anything, just as long
as it came from my hands.

No dice.

Another ghost?
That had to be it! Yes there was, only one, but it was big, real big, like 5 foot 2 big with blonde hair and a Queen's accent. I ransacked my apartment for the ghost's phone number, found it and picked up the phone, screamed: PREPARE TO BE EXCORCISED YOU ROTTEN MOTHER, punched the 11 digits and waited
for the
ghost voice.

"Hello?"

"Guess who baby."

"John?"

"That's right John, I was calling to tell you that I've cleaned up my act, 100 percent! No more booze or drugs, and guess what,

I'm an investment banker now, suit and tie, clean shave, making the real cash, 100 plus a year."

"Oh yeah John. You're an investment banker, I believe that alright."

"But I am. I'm working for one of the Big Boys downtown. I've got my own office and everything. In fact, I'm looking over some paperwork right now, serious stuff, too; purchase agreements, holding options, maturity dates."

"John, did you forget something?

"What do you mean?"

"John, I know you. I know how you are. You can't really expect me to believe all that."

"But it's the truth." A section of newspaper had somehow escaped the flames; I picked it up and rattled the pages by the mouthpiece. "You hear that baby. That's the sound of documents. Important documents! I'm a closer! I'm making deals right now!"

"No you're not. I can just imagine what you're doing right now. You're probably sitting on your couch in boxer shorts and that Burroughs t-shirt with the cigarette burns (I was). You're probably drinking cheap beer and writing bad poems (it's true). I wouldn't be surprised if you were jerking off." (SHIT!)

I took my hand out of the opening of my shorts and hung up the phone. I was getting nowhere with this. The words just wouldn't come. Shit! I couldn't even come! SHIT!
I picked up the phone and threw it across the room.
I stood up and kicked a hole in the wall.
I smacked empty bottles from the coffee table and sent them crashing across the floor.
I was in a rage so I
started after the television and I remember thinking:

This has to be the root of all my problems! This idiot box had turned my brains to jelly. There must be some type of rays that blast out of the screen and work directly on the creative center of my mind. Of course! Why would those network bastards want me thinking on my own? That has to be it! I must destroy the rays! DEATH
TO THE RAYS!!!

I screamed that last line and flung myself at the monitor, full speed, cocked back for the right hook, released it. Kuushh! And the side panel dented inward. I yanked the plug from the wall, lifted the television set above my head and walked towards the window. I was going to be free of the rays! Once I finished the job I would be free! Free to write without network rays screwing up my thought process!
FREE!

I rested the weight of the television on the window ledge
looked down on the empty street,
counted:
1,
2,
3
and
re-
lease. The set went out, flipping end over end through empty space, the cord sailing behind it like a black tail and the crash was LOUD, the screen smashing into a thousand pieces on the street below, vacuum tube guts spilling across the pavement like the aftermath scene of some robot war. Wires and chips (and don't forget that fucking transponder responsible for the rays) lay destroyed and scattered on the sidewalk.

After surveying the damage, I began to relax. What I had done was good. It had purpose. I took a deep breath, exhaled and whispered, very soft, to the ruins on the street: Free, I'm finally fucking free of you.

I turned from the window, looked around the room and studied my work. (Not bad, not bad at all John, you sure are one tough bastard, you deserve a beer for all your hard work - that's right baby I do deserve a beer and furthermore I am a tough bastard, mind you don't forget that) I went back to the desk carrying a bottle of domestic beer, sat in front of *The Machine* and pulled up a blank page. My mind felt clean, my heart rate was up and any minute now the words were going to march across the screen.

I SAID
ANY MINUTE
NOW . . .

GOD
DAMNIT! No dice. I stared at the page.
How I hated all that white space.
It just sat there, mocking me,
daring me to lay down the lines trapped in my head.
I yelled at the screen:

"C'mon you bastard. Don't you know I have to meet this
deadline? FUCKING PRODUCE!"

No answer.
No dice.
No words!
No -
Shit! NO DICE!

Then I saw what the problem was; the stereo.

Now that had to be it.
Why, there's probably a transponder lodged in the guts of that
thing. That transponder could be pumping out the rays just as the
television did. Maybe even more deadly and more potent,
omnipotent type rays! I jumped away from the desk, ran over to
the wall unit that housed the lethal, ray sending stereo and pulled
it free from the shelf. I ran to window, holding the stereo and
letting it know: end of the line buddy, its
curtains for you!

The stereo joined the television on the street. I still wasn't
satisfied. You see, these network guys, they're crafty bastards.
They could stick those damn transponders in anything, why, that
toaster could be a cold, hard, thought killing machine! Goodbye.
The answering machine might accommodate an amplifier that
increases the signal strength of the rays! Take it easy old chum.
The can opener and blender, my electric razor and the battery
operated toothbrush! So long guys.
The vcr and my wristwatch, every remote control in the place, all

of it! Sianarra! Hasta
Luego!

5 stories below, the street was a mess. (and surprisingly, no one
had called the police yet) A hundred different pieces of a
hundred different ray-transmitting machines were scattered on
the pavement. Batteries and cords mixed with glass and circuit
boards, diodes and tubes, all this shit, all these things that I had
stolen or bought or found, all of them, all filled with the
network's deadly transponders and they all
were dead.

Freedom.

I went back to *The Machine*, now it crossed my mind that there
could be a transponder in *The Machine* itself. Why wouldn't
there be? Those fuckers are crafty; they could've thrown one in
there at any given time without me knowing.

Maybe I should destroy that as well?

I went to work on pulling the cord from its outlet. Once this last
transponder was taken care of I'd really be able to lay it down.
No questions asked, the words would pour like wine across the
page and read like Fante when I was done, I knew it! But on my
way to the window,
I saw the real problem.

Oh,
you
bastard, you horrible, rotten mother,
hiding like that so that I wouldn't see you, oh, you fucking scum
have I got your number, oh yes your number, right
here baby - and it took less than two minutes
to destroy
that dirty
evil mirror, I plugged *The Machine*
back into the wall
drank four beers and
typed out this column.

broken bottles in the corner of the room (steps)
1 razor and some powder on a mirror (to)
an insane blonde lying on my couch (the)
mirror asks where I'm headed (madhouse)

- pornography, while picking roses -

skeleton in my closet shakes
hands with a mannequin (steps)
a blow-up doll filled with helium (to)
the ceiling can be scraped for resin (the)
phone rings:
Will you accept a collect call
from Dr…
(madhouse)?

- .45 revolvers,
and an early morning deathbed -

cat claws at my insides (steps)
the broken alarm clock shattering space (to)
my kitchen table covered in blood (the)
mailman brings my acceptance letter:
Mr.
Dempsey,
we are pleased to announce that you
have been chosen for the prestigious…
(madhouse)

- snake tongue,
forked at the sky in A minor -

fly fishing off the fire escape (steps
in my window dressed in all black) to
(that summer I met Melanie,
when she let me put my hand up her shirt
and I felt (the)) weight of mescaline
pulling me towards the concrete (steps
and I looked across the long island sound (to) make sure there

were no other boats in
(the) water but
my own, my
own and when I turned
back
(madhouse)

# From *The Progress Of Ants*

## ℭℜ NATURAL BORN

Kid, you just weren't built to win this game
every day
a defeat in itself
you wake up and lose
open your eyes and its all over
look in the mirror and you're a missing person

but every
now and then
it feels as if you get lucky
some small victory is tossed from the pack
you catch the train
make a light
maybe lay a good piece of ass without too much work and at a
damned reasonable price . . .

it happens
every
now and then
but

maybe every now and then
just isn't good enough.

## ✺ I Had Just Been Out For A While And When I Came To ... I

stumbled towards the bathroom like a canary
escaping a cage
escaping a coal mine
with deadly fumes round my head
muddling my thoughts
muddling my sense

and I felt along the wall (in the dark) for my toothbrush (in the
dark;
I
had used the last of my light bulbs, 8 in all, had
strung them from the ceiling with fishing line and tossed butter
knives (target practice) at them until I considered myself a
menace) eventually

I found it,

the toothbrush, but the bristles were wet and I yelled out:

"Who the fuck's been using my battery operated appliances?"

and then memory kicked in
reminded me that I was alone,
house empty, also
that I hadn't been brushing my teeth, strange,
going on three days now, showerless, soapless, lifeless and
useless . . . (I hadn't even
been outside,
just the bathroom and the kitchen and the bedroom,

vomiting, eating, drinking beer while jacking off across a white
screen I

it

the writing process,

sure . . .)
then somehow I found the toothpaste,

and there was a candle held in place
by a pool of dried wax on the counter top,
and a book of matches
and half a cigarette,
and I lit all three,
screaming:

"Let there be light in this cunt dark abyss!"

and it worked,
the mirror caught the reflection and now
I had 2 candles burning;
a producer,
a scientist,
a genius I was and there were two of me, the genius, in that
bathroom,
each being illuminated by that candle,
and one of them smiled, showing yellow teeth
and a grin
fit
for four white walls . . .

smile caused that half cigarette to drop out of my face,

thing singed my nipple hairs on the way down,
caught my belly,
top of my foot,
red embers,
I bent down to pick it up,
forehead against the counter with a thud, candle tipped pouring
hot wax down my legs, arms swung out instinctively, knocking
everything off the counter, I
howled and lost balance,
hit the tiles with a dead swan grace and looked
around at the enclosing darkness,

no way I could find my toothbrush in all this . . .

I crawled back into the bedroom,
made it into bed,
I felt nauseous, head ringing,

pain from all over and I
still hadn't brushed my teeth . . .

tomorrow . . .

I closed my eyes and
passed out
thinking of canaries,
cages and coal mines.


## ℭℛ Excuse Me Sir,
### It Seems As If Our Navigator Has Misplaced The Map . . .

All these lights
All these cars
All these people
Operating all these machines
It makes me wonder
If any of them know where they're going
It makes me wonder
If any of them are as lost as I am . . .

Sometimes I'll think about the future
And the only things I can see
Are more people
Operating more machines
Or maybe even
Vice versa
And when I see myself
I'm still on the street corner
Just looking at all the lights
And at all the cars
And wondering if any of the people
Are as lost as I am

## ❧ WHERE

and she asks me if I drink absinthe because of Hemingway
and I let her know

big sister I've got problems

skin peeling and stomach pains
shaky hands and dead ends
haven't fought my way out of the paper bag
still stuck in the cocoon

mind is a wild card
and I'm surprised that I know your name
numb as numb can be
I'm just floating around here

flotsam and jetsam
wasted time and debris
sue hess, renee angers
throw me a fucken life raft

1970's television
and a 3com cable modem
I should be out west
typing novels, screwing blondes
I should be in Florida
catching marlin and mahi-mahi
I should be anywhere
except for here . . . big sister,

I'm just screwed

## ❧ SENSELESS BEGINNINGS

barely getting started
and already
I've written too much; too many words, too many lines, too
many cheap poems

about hotel rooms gone bloody
and a homespun rocket
that just won't lift off:

futility -
frustrating as jacking off under a cold shower,
frustrating as jacking off under a cold shower in a public
bathroom, middle of a
foreign country,
place reeks of
sexual deviancy
and the mold grouted
with tile spores, and from outside
comes alien language,
and the sound
explodes
upstairs
into alien image, while keeping rhythm
and these actions,
these actions allow a man to laugh
in the face of desperation


## ❧ THE INEVITABLE JOHN

I was meant for broken teeth
back alleys
and dark bars
carnivals and subways
someplace stale

I was meant for dreams of sour milk
old soda and young death
smoking cigarettes and drinking
in a parked car watching a fishing dock

I'm just no good with leather chairs
and multi-colored lights make me anxious

I want change for a ten
when ordering 2 beers

Mama

give me an old stool
and a television
with the volume
way down
and I'll be content
not to yell
or throw bottles
across the room


## ☙ A MAN OF VISION

(She asked me and I thought for a moment . . .)

Waiting to grow tits and lose hair
Waiting for ulcers, hemorrhoids, cancer and the clap
Waiting for lung, liver, kidney and heart disease
Waiting to start dialysis,
AA,
who knows,
jail time
Waiting to get married
so that I can turn around
and get divorced *Why,*
*that whore took half my empire!*
Waiting for hernias, social security, pension plans
Waiting to wear diapers *Nurse,*
*I've had an accident.*
Waiting for 2 pills to take effect and it's just not happening
*Fuck! Ah!*
*Generics!*
Waiting for tax returns, paychecks, fan letters and fame
Waiting for the planet to explode
Waiting on the next train
Waiting for happy hour - beer drunk

leering, there's this real easy one
sitting next to me,
crossing legs, back and forth, the thigh's lifting, each time
a little higher, each time
showing a little more skin and she puts a cigarette between
bloody
red-tinted
lips,
sucks on the thing like a pro, exhales
and asks, "So,
what're you waiting for?" and I tell her,
"Not a thing kitten,
not a god damned thing."

## ℭℜ THE FASHIONABLE MARTYR

man'll sacrifice himself for anything
for jobs and cars
and boats and pools
for houses on the water
and women with legs
man'll open his veins
and bleed across floors
lie in pools of warm water
and listen to his heart
to secure a big screen television
and a week in the Caribbean
man'll loop a rope around his neck
and swing from 9 to 5 rafters . . . and while getting dressed for
work
in the morning I expect to hear
heavy police issued footsteps
climbing the stairs . . . there's a law in this state
something against suicide

but I just don't get it

## CUNT STUCK IN APRIL

shit rings around the toilet
I think I've fallen for another woman

works like this:
she's still a mystery
little girl barely knows me
and that's what makes it right, and special
that's what makes it beautiful, drinking beer on a Saturday
morning,
lusting after a stranger,
I didn't get any sleep last night . . .

## AH, SPRING

she rubbed foot powder into her bush
and sprinkled vinegar across her toes
he mixed sperm with melted wax
and spelled out his name on the counter top
without a word
without a plan
just matching
Check Engine lights
they took off down the road
heading someplace

warm